Mercy's Gate

KITTY WEVER

Mercy's Gate

Copyright 2019 by Kitty Wever
Kitty Wever Publishing

Contact the author at: KittyWeverPublishing@gmail.com

Printed in the United States of America

ISBN 978-0-578-53407-7

Chapter 1

"Oh, no! it's positive!" Megan whispered. "Maybe I did something wrong." Rereading the instructions on the box, she went through the list. The strip definitely showed positive. Three weeks late and her period was never late. *There's no way I could be pregnant*, she reasoned. *It just happened that once.*

"Megan, it's almost 7:30," her mom called from the kitchen.

Racing through the kitchen, she grabbed a piece of toast and her backpack for school. She had to avoid any eye contact or conversation with her mom.

"Honey, you've got to eat more than a piece of toast." Rita Latham objected.

"I'll be fine, Mom. I've got to get to school."

Closing the door behind her, Megan breathed a sigh of relief at escaping her mom's watchful eye and questions. Just as quickly, she felt the panic return. She ran to the bus, as if running might provide some kind of relief.

Collapsing into a seat on the bus, her mind reeled with confusion and fear. Memories of the afternoon Tony seduced her flooded her mind. It seemed totally surreal. Since then they had

3

barely talked to one another. She was completely baffled that it even happened. When they first met Tony had gone out of his way to bump into her and let her know he was interested. Since then he completely avoided her.

Megan had no idea the secret thoughts Tony experienced that day and since. He certainly hadn't planned it to happen. The time that afternoon at Chance's house was a crazy kind of memory for him too. Yes, his hormones were going crazy, but that was normal for a guy his age. But the surprise at his own level of irresistible sexual drive and Megan's submission to it was a complete shock. He couldn't stop himself, and yet it wasn't anything he planned.

Remembering how it all started that afternoon, Megan went from feeling normal to the point she couldn't and didn't even try to resist Tony. It sure wasn't because she felt physically turned on or anything. At the same time Tony was completely unrestrained and aggressive. As things progressed, she became more and more oblivious. It was as though she became a passive on-looker instead of the victim she was. She remembered Tony helping her get dressed when it was over, leading her out of Chance's house and then home. Sobering up as they walked to her house, she just wanted to get away from Tony and everything that happened.

As everyone piled out of the bus, she walked into school in a daze. Heading for her locker she moved ahead with steps into what could never be a normal day. Pulling out the books she needed for class and stashing her backpack, she closed her locker. Seeing Cherie approaching helped pull her into the moment. They had gotten to know one another over the last two years.

Feeling compelled to tell someone, Megan blurted, "Cherie. I need to talk to you."

"Sure, Megan. What's up?"

"You know the day I went with Tony over to Chance's house?"

"Yeah."

"Something happened that day between Tony and me."

"What do you mean something happened?"

"We were at Chance's hanging out and after a little while I started feeling really weird, like drugged or something. Chance and everyone else left Tony and I alone in his family room downstairs. Tony started coming on real strong. I felt like a rag doll, like I was stoned. I couldn't do anything to stop him. Next thing I knew my clothes came off and we were having sex."

Cherie's shocked look said it all. "What?"

"And that's not all. I did one of those pregnancy test strips this morning and I think I'm pregnant."

"You what?"

"I bought a pregnancy test kit from the store and did it this morning. It was positive. It said I am pregnant. I hardly remember how it happened. The day we were at Chance's house I think there was something in the drink Chance gave me or maybe Tony slipped something in it without my knowing it."

"Megan! You can't be serious!"

"Oh, yes I am."

"You're pregnant? And you think he drugged you?"

"Yes. I don't know. Like I said, maybe it was Chance. He and a couple other guys were there at first and started laughing about some private joke. I thought they were just acting stupid. After it was all over, Tony kept apologizing, saying he didn't mean for it to happen."

"What are you going to do?"

"I don't know. That's what I have to figure out."

5

"You've got to tell somebody."

"Who? I can't tell my folks. They would completely freak out! You know how they are."

"Maybe the test is wrong. What about the teen clinic on Brewster? I've heard lots of girls say they've gone there to get help. You know, like with birth control, and even with . . . abortions. They can at least tell you if the results you got are right."

"I don't know, Cherie! I don't know what to do. Maybe I'm not really pregnant. Maybe the results are wrong."

"Well, I know you can go there and find out. Your parents don't even have to know."

"I've got to get to class. Can you meet me after school so we can talk?"

"Of course, Megan. I'll meet you back here."

"Cherie, you can't tell anyone! Do you hear me? No one!"

"I won't, Megan. I promise."

"Okay, meet me back here after our last hour, okay?"

Chapter 2

Friday morning, and here she was at Albright Clinic. Megan had never been to a doctor or clinic without one of her parents. They always went out of their way to make her feel safe and protected. Especially her dad. Inside she shrank back from thoughts of him. She would be so ashamed for him to know. Her parents would probably love her in spite of everything, but why put them through it? And who knows how insane it would become if they thought she had been drugged by Chance or Tony. And what if they wanted her to keep the baby.

As she and Cherie entered Albright Clinic, Megan felt her legs about to give way. Cherie looked at Megan, feeling strangely out of place. She came as a support to Megan, but even though Megan had asked her to come, she suddenly felt pushed away, like an intruder.

Determined and strong, Megan wiped away her tears as if she would be just fine. Inside she was crying, *help me, God!*

The counselor at the clinic was right. After all, she was a professional and had helped so many other girls who found themselves in the same predicament. If she followed through with this pregnancy it would be nearly impossible to stay on the path to become a veterinarian. College and pursuing a career in veterinary medicine would be far more difficult, if not impossible. Then there was the whole thing of her parents and how it would affect them. Their friends and neighbors would no doubt be shaking their heads about what she was responsible for. She would definitely be causing their lives to change, and not for the better.

That day, the counselor asked, "Megan, shall we go ahead, make an appointment for you to have the procedure done and get you back to living life normally? We could have you back on track within just a week."

Refusing to think too long and hard and holding the emotions at bay, Megan caved and said, "Yes." What else could she do? Two days later here she was.

Stepping into the clinic, the receptionist, Louise, smiled broadly at Megan as she approached the check-in. Louise knew the clinic had a fairly busy day ahead. She was glad Megan was on time so things could move along. There were a total of eight procedures scheduled.

"Good morning, how can I help you?"

Megan nervously responded. "I'm Megan Latham. I have an appointment with Dr. Green."

"Yes, Megan. We have a few forms here for you to complete and sign. If you would like to have a seat and look them over. I'll let the doctor know you are here. It should be just a minute."

Looking over the day's schedule, Louise noted that although busy, this would be a shorter day than normal. Joseph Green had blocked out his availability from 4:00 p.m. to close that day. He left a note for her and Shirley Evans indicating he scheduled a business appointment, ending their day early. Louise and Shirley had become close friends, having worked together for well over six years. When Louise told Shirley their day would end at 4:00, both gave each other a look that said, "What is he up to?" Usually breaks in Dr. Green's schedule were booked right before lunch.

While Megan concentrated on the forms she was given to fill out, Cherie grabbed a few magazines and sat down beside her.

"Do you know how long this will take?" asked Cherie.

"No. They haven't told me, and I didn't ask the lady at the teen clinic."

The door separating the reception area from the patient rooms opened. Shirley Evans stood holding the door, and called her name. "Megan?"

Standing up, Megan thought she might keel over she felt so nervous.

Smiling confidently, Shirley put her at ease with a warm welcoming smile.

"Right this way, Megan. I'm Shirley Evans, Dr. Green's nurse. I'll be assisting with your procedure today."

Being well aware she was dealing with a very nervous teenager, Shirley Evans spoke as soothingly as possible. Entering patient room 3, Shirley motioned for Megan to enter.

"Megan, you look a bit nervous. We want you to relax as much as possible. You'll be just fine. The procedure is standard and one we perform routinely. There is no need to worry. Dr. Green and I will take good care of you. Change into this gown if you would and place your things in this locker. Once you are ready, just open the door a bit to let me know and I will be right in to get things started."

After changing into the hospital gown she sat down and waited for the nurse as instructed. The stirrups were a morbid reminder of what was about to take place.

Noting the signal of the door ajar, Shirley Evans knocked

and entered. "Megan, Dr. Green will be right in. Please take a seat here on the table, scoot back as far as you can, putting your head on the pillow. I'll help guide your feet into the stirrups. There we go. Comfortable?"

Megan nodded her head, responding in silence.

"Good. I'll cover you with this blanket so you don't get chilled."

The door opened and Joseph Green entered, introducing himself with a smile and handshake. "Good morning, Megan. I'm Dr. Green. Nurse Evans and I are going to take good care of you today. There is nothing to be anxious about. This is a procedure I and Miss Evans are both very familiar with. It won't take long at all. She will administer a medication to help you relax. We will begin as soon as you're ready. The only thing we need you to do is close your eyes and lay back."

The foreign sounds, and methodical progression of motions and instructions to Nurse Evans seemed strangely detached from her, and yet it was Megan's own body that was the center of the activity. The indignity of nakedness and physical contact with her body by these complete strangers to her life was so embarrassing to her, but mechanical and unnoticed by them. Megan somehow detached mentally. Her thoughts flashed back to Tony. She had heard other girls and women mostly on television and in movies talking about sex being so amazing. That sure wasn't the case for her. Tony may have been experiencing physical pleasure that day, but she hadn't. In fact she not only didn't think it was so great, it seemed down right crazy and disgusting. And now this!

Joseph Green's voice interrupted her thoughts, "We're nearly done here, Megan. Just a few last details and we'll be finished. You did great."

Continuing with their motions and instructions, it was

evident Shirley Evans and Joseph Green were simply carrying out a familiar routine. A tray of instruments was the focus of their activity, each being handed first to the doctor and then back to Shirley after use.

Joseph Green silently gave Nurse Evans a knowing nod toward another tray on wheels nearby. She pulled it over and stood in such a way as to block Megan's view. Joseph Green was lifting something and transporting it into some type of package on top of the tray. Nurse Evans surveyed the contents carefully and gave him a nod as acknowledgment as if to say everything was accounted for. Unaware that Nurse Evans was literally accounting for all body parts, Megan was alarmed to realize it was already over. The medical terminology exchanged by doctor and nurse served as a barrier separating her from the physical reality of the moment. The final clatter of instruments being gathered and placed aside loudly brought the activity to an end.

What Megan had no knowledge of was that each set of remains was placed and preserved in prescribed packaging to be picked up by a surgical service each day from the clinic. Joseph Green wasn't exactly sure what the final procedure was after being picked up, but had been reassured when he signed the contract for sterile handling that they would be removed and properly handled.

Overtaken with a sense of wrongdoing, a cry rose from deep within Megan. "Stop!" she cried. "Where's my baby?" Megan asked.

Ignoring her question, Shirley purposefully avoided eye contact. As she pushed aside the cart with the plastic surgical container near the bed, Megan retorted, "Is that where you put it?"

Nurse Evans turned her head away and closed her eyes.

"Megan, everything went well and there is nothing for you

11

to do now but rest and relax." Her voice was calm and unyielding to Megan's mild hysteria.

"Why don't you answer me? Is that where you put my baby?"

Dr. Green stepped back, pulling off his surgical gloves.

"Megan, I realize this can seem like a very difficult thing emotionally, but everything went fine. Nurse Evans here will be taking good care of you."

Shirley Evans had learned long ago to just keep moving and not get caught up in overthinking what was taking place or any of the emotional upheaval that sometimes resulted. As she looked at Megan, she thought, *Oh, if these kids would only learn to use birth control!*

Overwhelmed with shame and guilt, Megan thought, *My God, what have I done?*

Finishing the cleanup, Shirley was shocked to see Megan attempting to get up, and she gently restrained her.

"Megan, you must not try to get up right now. It's important that you rest. I'll check with Dr. Green to see what we can give you to help with that."

She eased her hold, making sure the teen wasn't still fighting to get up. Getting this girl out of here and into another room was paramount. After wheeling Megan out of the surgical room and into a quiet side room, Shirley breathed a sigh of relief. "I'll be right back. Please do not try to get up. Just lay back and relax."

Megan's head fell back into the pillow. *Oh my God! How can this be happening?*

Coming in with a syringe in hand, Shirley approached and swabbed Megan's hip. "Dr. Green has approved a mild sedative to help you relax. He wants you to take time to rest. If you are in pain, let us know and we will get you something."

"When can I go?"

"We'd like you to rest for at least a couple of hours to make sure everything is okay. The pull cord is right here if you need anything. We will continue to check on you."

"Do you ever wonder about what you do here? Does it ever bother you?"

"Megan, I've learned that sometimes we have to make difficult choices. I'm sure the counselor you met with at the clinic talked with you about this."

"But, what if it really is as wrong as people say? What if God thinks it's wrong?"

"Well, I guess I'll have to leave that up to God. In the meantime, we have helped many women in very difficult situations in life."

Giving in to the sedative, Megan drifted off.

She awoke, startled at the time. It was nearly 1:00. She had to get going. No point waiting for someone to come in. Still slightly light-headed, Megan got up to dress, bracing herself to keep from falling. Ignoring the instructions to wait for assistance, she got dressed, tied her shoes and headed out. Following the exit signs, the door opened to the reception room. Coming face to face with Cherie, she flushed with embarrassment having forgotten Cherie was even there.

"I thought you were never going to be done, Megan. Are you okay? Did you know it was going to take this long?"

Cherie's complaint was the last thing Megan could deal with at this point. Right away Cherie dropped her gaze, knowing Megan was not okay.

Alerted earlier by Shirley Evans that Megan was really distraught after the procedure, Louise Blake stood up behind the reception desk, knowing they weren't quite ready to see Megan leave.

"Megan, there are some instructions here we need to review with you before leaving the clinic. Please have a seat and I'll get someone to help you."

Megan rolled her eyes. She could barely restrain herself. "I just want out of here. I want to go home."

Cherie tossed the magazine she'd been reading and jumped up, ready to follow Megan out. It was obvious Megan wasn't doing well. Feeling awkward but concerned, Cherie said, "You look really upset. Did everything go okay?"

"If that's what you call okay," Megan quipped.

Returning after quickly notifying Shirley that Megan was already dressed and ready to walk out, Louise handed Megan a clip board with a form to complete.

"Dr. Green asked that you review this Release Form and sign it before leaving today," Louise said.

After skimming over the instructions and signing the release, Megan handed the clipboard back to Louise, and turned to go.

As soon as the door closed behind them, Shirley stepped into the Reception Room and shaking her head said to Louise, "I swear, these girls blow my mind. You'd think they would learn."

Hearing the elevator bell announce its arrival, Megan breathed a sigh of relief when the doors opened. As she and Cherie stepped on silence fell. Internally they both wanted to just get away from this place and each other. Glad no one else was on the elevator, Cherie warily glanced Megan's way. Megan simply stared ahead.

Stopping at an intermediate floor, a woman holding a baby stepped on, brushing lightly against Megan. Her eyes went immediately to the baby. *What a beautiful baby!*

The mother smiled and cooed, brushing its cheek with her hand. "Mommy's right here, pretty girl."

When the elevator came to a final stop, the doors opened and Cherie followed the mother and child into the lobby. Megan seemed frozen in time, her eyes following the woman and baby as they disappeared from view. *Oh my God, what have I done?* she silently cried within.

"Coming?" asked Cherie. "We could get something to eat. I'm starving!"

How can you be so oblivious to what I just went through? You are clueless! You don't even seem to care what just happened to me, thought Megan.

"No. I'm not hungry. They told me I'm supposed to go home and rest. I don't want to go anywhere but home."

"You sure?"

"Yeah. I'll just catch a bus here and go home."

"Okay. Get some rest. I hope you feel better. It'll be okay, Megan. At least it's over."

Walking away, Megan knew in her heart this would never be over. She would relive this time in her life over and over. Just then her cell phone rang.

"Hey, Megan! It's Tony."

"What do you want?" Megan replied.

"Megan, what's wrong? Where are you?"

"Do you really want to know?" She hadn't told him she was pregnant. It seemed like he was just someone who was busy avoiding her. Disconnected and uncaring.

"I didn't see you in school."

"Well, you'll love to hear this. I was pregnant, Tony. And I actually just left Albright Abortion Clinic. I got rid of the baby,"

"What?"

"You heard me. I was pregnant and I got rid of it."

"Why didn't you tell me?"

15

"Since when did you want to talk to me again? Every time I see you you head in the other direction. And what exactly would you do about it? You're the one that made this happen."

"Megan, I don't even know how it all happened. It's weird, but somehow it felt like I was drunk or drugged when we did what we did at Chance's. Chance was laughing the next day at school and said something about how he hoped we enjoyed the drinks he gave us."

"That's exactly what I mean. I knew you would just freak out like this. Don't worry. It's over, Tony! The baby is gone! Now just leave me alone." Hanging up, she hoped this would really be the end of it all. None of this was what she wanted.

Chapter 3

"Mom, I'm home." called Megan.

The surprised look on her mom's face approaching from the kitchen reassured Megan she still had no clue as to what was going on.

"Hi, honey. You're home early. Really early! It's only 1:30. Are you okay?"

"Not really."

"What's the matter?"

"I just don't feel good. I need to lie down for a while."

"Why? What's wrong? You look awful. Have you been crying?"

"I'll be okay. I just need to go to bed. Just sort of lightheaded and sick to my stomach."

"Oh, oh. I hope you're not coming down with the flu or something. The Petersons are coming for dinner tonight, remember."

"I just need to lie down."

"Would you like me to pray for you?"

"No, I'll be fine."

"You've been so tired lately. Maybe I should make an appointment for you to see Dr. Jorgenson. Make sure there isn't something going on."

That thought struck like a thunder-bolt. Dr. Jorgenson was the last person she needed to see right now. Then everything would be exposed!

"Okay Honey. Go upstairs and lie down. I'll come up in a little while to check on you."

Each step up to her room seemed to make the abdominal cramps she felt worsen. Quickly closing the door behind her, she sighed with relief. Her parents thought she was so innocent. Boy, would they be shocked to know the truth.

She tugged at her clothes to pull them off. Slipping into pajamas, hoping to find some relief she flopped into bed. Flashes of the beautiful baby on the elevator kept coming to mind.

The counselor at Planned Parenthood was so nice and seemed so wise at the time. But none of what they had talked about addressed this feeling of utter loss and regret.

Embracing her beautiful but old and worn out stuffed bear, Edward, caused her to yearn for the peace and comfort she always knew as a child. It was somehow gone and replaced with a sense of hopelessness and permanent separation from that safe haven of innocence.

Megan's cell phone rang. Reaching to pick it up, she hesitated as she answered.

"Hey, Cherie!"

"Hi, Megan. Guess what? You're never going to believe this. Sandy Thurston is pregnant and her mom is telling her she has to have the baby! Can you believe it? Megan. Are you there?"

"I gotta go." Megan replied. She hung up and began to weep uncontrollably and loudly.

The door opened with her mother's tapped announcement.

"Megan!" Rita Latham gasped.

Crying uncontrollably, Megan burst. "Oh Mom."

"Megan, what is it? What's wrong?"

18

Chapter 4

"Amy Ferguson, remember you're the girl that has it all together," she said out loud to herself. Friends, both male and female were constantly telling her that. In one way or another they told her she was one of the strongest people they'd ever known. Straight-forward in her thinking and her living. Undaunted by what many thought was not only boldness but brashness. "Independent" could be her middle name. Instead, it was May. Amy May Ferguson. She always thought it sounded strong. Of course only she knew how vulnerable she could really be. She learned to be tough as the youngest of five girls. One sister always treated her cold, calling her a brat, while the other three seemed oblivious to anything being wrong. She had the sense of being on her own, having to step up to the plate in life to take care of herself, even at home. As a result she had vowed to do just that, no matter what. Her dad had died when she was five, and her mother was too busy working to take care of them to notice Amy's feeling of estrangement. Her older siblings resented the fact that she was the youngest, always complaining she was spoiled.

Feeling the key insert and turn, she breathed a sigh of relief. Home finally! Her appointment had been at 1:00 that afternoon at Albright Clinic. She wouldn't have thought she'd get home this late. Stripping off her clothes, she became physically aware of what she had just put her body through. The pain med and anesthetic were wearing off. An abortion. She never thought this would happen. So much for birth control.

She was taken back by the teenage girls who were on their way out of the clinic as she entered. Silently, she mused how little they really knew about how to manage in life, all the while believing they knew so much. If they knew even the half of it when it came to life, they never would have been there. After all, she was at least ten years older and she had made so many mistakes they couldn't be counted. Having been told there was only a 2 percent chance she could get pregnant, she foolishly believed this would never happen. And yet there she was, the 2 percent!

Her *aloneness* dogged her daily. Here she was with a beautiful custom-decorated condo from entry to rear and yet there was no one to enjoy it with. No one to greet or be greeted by when coming home. No confidant to share her deepest secrets with. *No shoulder to cry on.* No one she could just be herself with. This very independence admired so by others held her prisoner to a life that had taken on a psychological duality. One moment she felt in complete control, and then the next she'd find herself feeling depressed and completely powerless in the self-constructed vacuum she hid within.

As a call girl, shame and self-disgust were her constant companions; relentlessly encroaching and harassing her as she allowed herself to be used by men for their revolting lusts. She detested every moment she allowed them to take advantage of her. And yet she was the very one who gave them permission to violate and degrade her. No matter how she tried to rationalize what she did, there was no escape from the stench of it.

And now, with what she had chosen to do today, she had backed herself into yet another self-sabotaging corner. *Really, Amy? What were you supposed to do? Have a baby?* For sure she had no choice in this matter. Selling her body to any and every disgusting man with the necessary money made the idea of a baby impossible. *Yeah right, like I'm going to have a baby and be a mother?*

Deep inside she was shaken by a small voice saying, *"But why couldn't you be my mommy?"*

"Okay, these thoughts have got to stop! I've got to get high!' Continuing with her self-dialogue she sternly quipped, "You didn't have a choice. After all, you know there's no way you can earn enough to take care of yourself and a baby too. There's no way you could go to college, work full time, AND raise a baby! No way. Besides, what would you have told the baby and everybody else? Who was the father? You'd just say, "'I don't know.'"

Lying in bed, smoking some weed, she stared at the ceiling. Flipping on the TV in the hopes of finding a diversion, a diaper commercial came on.

She stood up, threw the remote, and shouted, "Stop it!" as if she was talking to an accuser standing by.

There aren't any bridges back. Who are you kidding? You've burned them all. The bridge into a life that she condemned along with everyone else. Prostituting herself. And for what? The constant banter back and forth within was like a tennis match with herself. And now more fuel poured on the fire! Taking the life of a baby. Somehow the ongoing wrong choices and decisions were catapulting her into a state where life was way beyond control.

You've really done it now! Bad enough you're a hooker. Now this. You don't care about anything or anyone anymore.

21

Sitting in front of the mirror in her apartment, she was drowning in the rubble of her broken dreams and scarred memories. Somehow every time hope of any kind arose, it vanished. She wasn't really in control. She was trapped in an existence few, if any, could escape. Contaminated and dirty, she knew no decent man would ever want her.

She thought of the day she first went for a consultation at Dr. Green's clinic. When asked about the father of the child she carried, and if the issue of abortion had been discussed, she immediately lied.

"Yes, of course, but the decision was left up entirely up to me."

She wasn't about to tell him she didn't know who the father was. It was none of his business. In fact, even if she knew which man it was, he wouldn't want it. Quite the opposite.

With tears welling up in her eyes, she grabbed the prescription bottle the clinic had issued. Swallowing three without reading any instructions, she then glanced at the label. One every four to six hours. Knowing her tolerance level for barbiturates, she shrugged off the over indulgence. She had to shut this off and get some sleep somehow. There was no way she was going to stay awake and listen to any more of this. She knew well enough by now that she'd drive herself crazy thinking about it all. Pouring a drink of scotch she chugged it down.

As much as she fought the feelings and thoughts about those she had physically touched and vehemently despised, she cried out with every ounce of her being for a man to love her and care for her. One she could truly love and care for and who would devote himself to her. All she had was a string of men who wanted a "piece" of her, leaving a used carcass behind. Not only did none of them care, they were more than willing to take part in her destruction.

For a while there had been a sense of control in her about those she surrendered her body to. She had something they could only acquire with money. Most of them were too old and unattractive to find women on their own, or they had wives at home whose legal rights in marriage forced the men to enter into acts with women who posed no threat to them as long as they kept their identities secret. And yet, that control Amy sensed was continuously dashed when she entered into acts that totally humiliated her. Yes, she could demand their money but somehow what they took in exchange from her was something worth so much more than they ever paid.

Looking in the mirror at the train wreck her life had become, she quipped, "What's the use? Look at you. You're nothing and no one will ever want you. You'll grow old alone. No good man could ever want you. And now you've even destroyed your own child. You might as well just give it up? Nothing's ever going to change. You've destroyed your life and you'll never get it back."

I'd like to just curl up and die, she thought. *But that's not going to happen unless I make it happen. How about some pills? I can call Jim and have him get me something. If I take enough, I'll be a goner for sure.*

Pondering suicide, the question arose within, *Who cares if I'm dead or alive?*

Her family had made it crystal clear time and again they didn't understand her and weren't interested. Her mother was now a hopeless alcoholic married to a man she'd met just a few years before Amy graduated high school. Her step-dad was a loser who continued chasing other women. He paid for the house they lived in, all the booze her mother could drink, and if that wasn't good enough he made it clear she could leave. *Mom sure doesn't seem to care about me, so why should I,* Amy mused.

Looking back at her life and all the relationships she'd had, there was only one who she believed really cared. Jared. They had been high school sweethearts, but then were separated when his family moved to the East Coast. His father had gotten a better job. They'd lost contact, even though she always believed they belonged together. She saw him on Facebook with other girls' names always popping up. Finally she had resigned herself to never seeing him again. No one else came along in time who cared like he had.

"Enough!" she said to herself, reaching for her phone.

"Hello."

"Hi, Jim? This is Amy."

"Hey Amy, how are you doin'?"

"Okay. I...I need some barbs. Do you have anything?"

"Sure, sweetie. How many do you need?"

"Oh, I don't know. Three dozen, I suppose."

"When do you need them?"

"Now."

"Okay. Give me a minute to make contact and I'll get right back to you."

"Thanks, Jim."

"Sure. No problem. Talk to you in a minute."

"Bye."

As she sat holding the receiver she silently wished he would have noticed something in her voice, and yet she felt restrained from betraying herself. The isolation she felt was intensifying more and more with each passing moment. Images of Innocent babies filled her mind, and then became gruesomely torn and maimed. Putting both hands to her ears, she fought to keep the thoughts from entering. Tears streamed down as they continued to barrage her.

Her own mind was a battlefield. She craved for someone to

break through all the walls that enclosed her, and yet she felt totally incapable of reaching out to anyone.

She was just a discarded tramp in a heap of society's rejects. Those in her profession lived within their own self-erected penitentiaries. Their hurts and hungers were buried deep under the scar tissue of life's circumstances. Any personal vulnerability to another was determinedly hidden. The cardinal rule was never expose your real self to anyone. Hold it all inside. All the hurts. All the disappointments. All the abuses. All the pain. All the suffering. Keep the doors barred from letting anyone in. Even friendship for most of them was strictly defined and carried out to the extent of the other's usefulness. Whether to gain drug contacts, additional sources of business, paid protection by crooked authorities or whatever, fear and greed were their dictators. And to weaken any boundary of self-protection only led to potential points of entry and attack. Games were played with all those around, the games of survival of the fittest. And the fittest were always the most cunning and ruthless. To win you had to be able to refuse any thoughts of respect or concern for others. Crazy as it seemed, the importance of the entire struggle was vanishing in her mind. None of it mattered anymore.

"Why am I living this way? I always wanted the same kind of life other women have. Why couldn't I live the same way they do? I did have choices. And I made all the wrong ones."

Avenues chosen seemed to be the only sure way to get ahead. But somehow nothing ever worked out the way she intended. Every time she thought she was getting ahead, something went wrong and she was back behind the same eight ball. Back into the same losing position. Something was always stealing the dream, and so the cycle continued.

Then entered a thought she had never before contemplated.

This life can't be worked out of. It can only be stepped out of. "If I could step out of this mess, wouldn't I do it?" she answered out loud.

The silence that came bounding back was overwhelming.

"Oh God. What am I supposed to do? Why even bother living? Why try to survive anymore? Who or what is it all for? Oh my God!"

She suddenly stopped and gazed at herself in the mirror.

"Yeah right, Amy. Now you're talking to God. What a joke. If there *is* a God, He wouldn't give you the time of day. Who are you kidding?"

She sat on her bed, grabbed two handfuls of hair, and began to yank and pull with all her strength. "You stupid slut. Why don't you just die?"

That single action graphically summed up her life…a self-made loser. Nothing she could or would do was ever going to change the course of her life. As in control as she tried to be, the more out of control everything was. She climbed out of bed and fell to her knees in utter sorrow and abandon. There was no more thinking life would ever be better. It was all over.

Staring off into space, suddenly a distant memory filled her mind…a Sunday morning when she went to church with a little friend in her neighborhood. She remembered how happy everyone was. It was as if God was reminding her of the message the teacher had shared.

For the first time since that day, she remembered the beautiful young Sunday school teacher said; "If you ever find yourself in a pit of trouble so deep, a place you can't find a way out of, always remember Jesus will save you. Pray and ask Him, He'll come and rescue you. He wants every one of you to know Him for who He is. And He wants to help. He came all the way down to earth to die for you to save you, so He could set you free. Always remember, He's just a prayer away. No matter what you've done or how bad things are, He loves you, and He will help you. He'll accept you just the way you are. He came to forgive your sins, all of them. So always remember there's nothing so terrible you can't find forgiveness and help in Him. All you have to do is ask for it. He loves you just the way you are."

Kneeling down, she made a decision within herself to challenge the course of her own future in a way she never thought possible.

"Jesus,' she began, "if You are real like that lady said, I'm in that pit. There's no way out. I don't know if You're real or not, or if any of this even matters anymore. I can't go on. I'm going to go to Jim's, pick up those pills, and end it all. I can't live like this anymore. If You're real, I need to know. If you did die for my sins, I've got thousands of them and I'm asking You to forgive me. If You really are God, then You see how many sins there are and how stinking rotten they are. If You can do anything to help, then I need You to show me. Otherwise I'm gonna end it all tonight. I can't take it anymore. Nobody cares about me, and frankly I don't care about myself. And if I'm just here talking to myself, then what does it matter anyway? It'll just go to show what I already know is true. Life isn't worth the pain. So I guess I'll leave it there and leave it up to You."

Standing up, she silently determined within herself that this was the end of it all. She had a true sense of resignation. She reached for the phone and redialed Jim's number.

"Hello."

"Jim, this is Amy again. Any luck?"

"Yeah, Amy. In fact I was just going to call you back. I'll

have them here within the hour. Why don't you stop by in about an hour and a half to pick them up?"

"Sounds good. I'll be there. That is, unless something comes up in the meantime."

"Oh, yeah, sure. I hear you. Well, if so just give me a call and I'll hold on to them for you."

She knew his response meant he thought that she might be called away on a "date." She wasted no energy explaining.

The decision had been made and she was going to move ahead with it.

"See you later," she replied, and hung up.

She got up and headed for the shower. *Might as well go out lookin' good*, she thought.

Walking down the hall, she was once again reminded of what her body had just been through. She slowed her pace and fixed her mind on her trip to Jim's. The drive would take about forty-five minutes, so she might as well get moving now. Feeling light-headed, she grabbed a chair back to steady herself. In the shower she continued to reaffirm within herself the decision she had made. The pills would make it final. There wouldn't be any need to worry about the future anymore.

Just as the baby's life had come to an end, so would hers. She remembered the three pills she had taken. Instead of feeling sleepy, the surge of adrenaline continued. The fact that she was so resigned to ending it all seemed to also bring an end to all the internal deliberations. The line was drawn. Only the follow-through mattered.

She stepped out of the shower and looked herself in the face in the mirror. She spoke out loud, "Well, Jesus, You have approximately an hour and a half to stop me. Otherwise, I'm gone."

Strangely, she regarded the decision as one weighing on

another's shoulders. Her desire and will to continue were no longer there. She just didn't care anymore.

Dressed to the hilt and steeped in perfume, she turned the lock on her apartment door to leave. She had a strong sense that her life as she had known it was over.

Chapter 5

Shutting the car engine off, Sheila breathed deep.

Thank God, it's finally over. Sheila, you did what you had to do, she reassured herself. *It was the right thing, and now you've just got to move on.*

Stepping out of the car, the sunlight disappeared into a slit across the bottom of the garage door. Thank goodness so many things were so simple. Push a button to open and close a garage door. No straining to do it herself. A life full of conveniences that made it so simple. Ending what would've been a very long and draining task. *Yes, that's what it was. Stopping a problem before it got started. Much better for me, Paul, and the boys . . . yes, even the baby. This old world is so full of problems; it's so much better off.*

Stepping into the kitchen, she could feel her cheeks flushing crimson when her eyes met Paul's.

"It's about time. Where have you been? I've been calling all over wondering if something happened. I keep telling you to call when you're going to be late so I won't worry."

"Don't you remember I told you this morning I had some things to do that would probably make me later than usual?"

"Oh, is that what you said? I was in such a hurry I guess I

30

didn't really pay attention. I had that meeting with Thompson this morning, remember? What a jerk. I keep telling him we're going to have some serious problems in production if we don't start listening to what the engineering guys are saying, but you'd think it was news to him. Anyway, I think he's finally going to call a meeting with them. How'd your day go?"

"Fine, why?" she retorted.

"Just wondering how your day went, that's all. Are you okay?"

"Of course I'm okay. Why wouldn't I be?"

"I don't know. You seem a little jumpy."

"Probably just the traffic on the interstate showing its profound effects on my emotions. Have you eaten dinner?"

"The kids were hungry, as usual, so we each had a sandwich. I'm sure we will still be hungry for dinner, whenever you have a chance to fix it."

"Would you mind terribly going out to get something? I don't think I have it in me to fix dinner tonight. I really need to lie down for a while."

"Are you sure you're okay, Sheila?"

"Maybe I better sit down for a minute. I'm a little lightheaded. Where are the boys?"

"They went over to Sean's house to play for a while." Paul paused, looking at her in concern.

"Sheila, maybe you better give up that job. You don't have to work, you know. Maybe it's more than you can handle."

"I can handle it," she snapped. "That job got us that boat you prize so highly, you know. And our checkbook is in a lot better shape. There's no way we could've done it without my job. You know that. We've had this discussion too many times, Paul."

"Yeah, I know. You don't have to get so defensive. I just don't want you overdoing it."

31

"Then help me more with the house and you won't have to worry about it. I thought you were in total agreement with me going back to work. Don't tell me we're going to consider my staying home again. I don't think I could handle that idea right now. Why are you bringing the subject up?"

"I don't understand. You keep telling me you're okay, you look as though you are about to faint, and you're getting uptight about everything I say to you. What's wrong, Sheila?"

"I'm sorry, Paul. It's been a long day. So many things are going on right now. I'm just tired."

"Okay, why don't you go rest? We'll talk after you get up."

Talking isn't what I had in mind, she thought. *Can't we just drop it?*

Riddled with guilt, she knew it was the secret she was hiding that caused her to draw back. She never had before. She never hid things from him. He always listened and at least tried to understand her position.

Sheila, remember what they told you. "This is your body. You have every right to determine what happens to it." Yes, but why don't I just tell him? Oh my God, why am I feeling like I'm lying to him about something that he has every right to know? After all, he is the father. It's something we created together, isn't it? Her mind reeled back and forth in confusion. *Why did it seem so right before, and now so confusing and deceptive?*

"Paul, I'm sorry I'm so irritable."

"Okay, Sheila, go ahead and rest. But we'll talk later to clear the air. There's some distance between us I don't like. If something is bugging you I want to know what it is. Okay?"

"Okay, Paul."

Escaping to their bedroom and closing the door behind her, she took a deep breath. The idea of keeping this to herself was more than she could deal with. She was fooling herself to think this could all be swept under the rug and forgotten.

There's no way you're going to be able to keep this from him, she said to herself. Sitting on the bed, she picked up the remote control and switched the television on. She had to get her mind on something else. Babies in a diaper commercial flashed before her. She quickly switched the channel, fighting back tears.

This is insane. What have I done?

The silence that enveloped the room caused the truth to scream even louder.

She impatiently rustled through her purse for the bottle of pain relievers, and angrily fumbled with the child safety cap.

"Take two every four to six hours as needed." She moved toward the bathroom to get a glass of water. Her strength was gone as she struggled to move in what felt like slow motion. She gulped down two of the pills, hoping relief would come from somewhere. Lying down, closing her eyes, she hoped sleep would come fast. She'd be more clear-headed when she woke up.

The only time in her life she could remember seeking an escape like this was when her father had died. It had happened when she was seventeen. They had been so close, and at the time she thought she'd never make it through the pain. It was as though a major piece of her existence was taken from her. He had been her rock, and the thought of going through life without him seemed unbearable.

The tears welled up in her eyes as the realization came. The emptiness she felt now as compared to then was in one way grievously different. What was cut off from her now was by her choice, unlike her father's death.

But why do both experiences feel so much alike?

Death in the family . . . there's been another death in the family, came the inward reply. She covered her face with her hands in

33

an appeal to stop her own thoughts. They refused to be ignored. Grief and self-condemnation seemed to be intertwined, pulling tighter around her mind. Hope was cut off; the hope she thought she was making possible.

What've you done to your family, Sheila? Did you really think you were doing them a favor? Or did you know deep down you were taking something away?

She heard Paul on the phone telling the boys to head home. Even though Bobby was only six and Evan eight, the thought of having to lie to them too filled her with dread.

Lying on the bed, struggling to bring the whirlwind within her mind to an end, she watched as Paul entered the room. As he looked at her, groping for understanding and insight, Sheila was unable to respond. The barrier erected through deception loomed. Silence was the only response she offered up.

"I don't know what's been going on with you the last couple of weeks, but you're acting really strange. You've been snapping at me and the boys for no reason. You're not communicating with me about anything, except what's for breakfast or dinner. I don't understand why. I'm beginning to think something is seriously wrong, and I want to know what it is."

She kept staring off in the opposite direction, unable to answer.

"I can't deal with this, Sheila. Whatever it is, let me in on it before it causes more problems between us."

Still no answer. The door slammed behind him.

Tears streamed down her face as the grief once again swept through her. *What am I doing? First I decide to get an abortion without telling Paul, so he won't have to deal with the question of it. And now I can't even tell him what I did.*

34

"Oh, God, what have I done?"

"Sheila," she heard Paul call out, "I'm going to take the boys to get something to eat."

"Okay." She was so drained of strength she couldn't say it loud enough.

"What?" Paul yelled.

"I said okay," she said again.

This time he faintly heard her. "C'mon boys, let's go."

"What's wrong with Mom?" asked Bobby.

"I'm not sure, sport. I'm trying to figure that one out myself. I guess she's not feeling real good. I think that job is more than she can handle. She'll feel better after she gets some rest. Let's go."

Sheila heard the car engine start and took a breath to relax. At least he wasn't there asking more questions. *What's he going to say? I thought it didn't matter as long as I kept it to myself and I didn't hurt anyone.*

Didn't hurt anyone! How about your own baby?

She got up from the bed, frantically seeking distraction. This was too much. These thoughts were going too far. Enough was enough.

"Get yourself together, Sheila. This is too much. You know you did what you had to do."

Walking past the mirror, she was startled by her own appearance. Unable to steady even her own thoughts, she realized everything had spun out of control.

"Sheila, you're an intelligent person. You know the person most closely affected by this would have been you . . . you made the right choice. You weren't ready for another baby, and you know it. And you kept it from having to go through all the pain and agony of this old world."

She curled up in bed and finally drifted off. Dreams of red and wrestling images filled her mind. Jolting awake when Paul entered the room, she sat up, trying to get her bearings.

"Paul, you're right. We need to talk. I had a scare. I had a pap smear that came back abnormal. I was afraid it was something really serious."

"And?"

"Well, the doctor said there were some precancerous cells and he said I need to stay on top of things and get rechecked every six months. I've just been nervous and I didn't want to scare you."

"Why didn't you tell me? I couldn't figure out what was going on. So everything's okay, sweetheart?"

"Yes. He just said we'd need to keep close tabs on it."

Well, this is a new feeling, she thought. *Guess I skated by this time. Thank God.*

"What's this? Something they gave you to take?" asked Paul, examining the prescription bottle on the nightstand. "Who's Joseph Green? I thought your doctor was Dr. Kelly."

"That's the doctor Dr. Kelly referred me to. He's a specialist. Dr. Kelly just wanted to make sure everything was okay."

"Why didn't you tell me, Sheila? Next time something like this happens, just let me know what's going on, would you?"

"I will, Paul. I promise. I just didn't want to worry you. Believe me, nothing like this will EVER happen again."

Chapter 6

"Hi, my name is Nancy Collier. I'm here to see Dr. Green." The receptionist's name tag let Nancy know this was the Louise she had spoken with on the phone before, the few times she had called his office.

"Thank you, Miss Collier. I'll let Dr. Green know you're here. Although I don't see you listed for an appointment with us."

"Well, it's actually an appointment I scheduled directly with him. Maybe he didn't enter it on your calendar."

Louise thought it was strange. They never scheduled anyone this late in the day. She thought she remembered hearing this woman's voice before, but she couldn't be sure.

"Please take a seat. I'll let Dr. Green know you're here."

Louise stepped into the back office. "Hey Shirley, do you know anything about an appointment scheduled for a Nancy Collier at 4:00 today?"

"Yes, Joe told me he was expecting someone. Not sure what it's about, but he said we could finish up and go home early."

"Well, I'm not asking any questions, if you know what I mean."

They exchanged a look. They had suspected for a long time that there was another woman in Joseph Green's life.

Unexplained calls and texts that would come during the day. He always stepped away into a private office to keep them from hearing. Although there was never an explanation, it didn't take a rocket scientist to know something was going on. She well knew his wife, Maggie's, voice. Louise and Shirley surmised long ago it wasn't a happy marriage. Half the time Maggie called into the office she sounded drunk. *How sad*, she thought.

"Okay. I'll let him know she's here. You can go ahead and lock up. Good night, Louise. I'll see you in the morning."

Louise excused herself, explaining to Nancy Collier that her day was over and the doctor would be right with her.

A few minutes later Shirley Evans entered the reception area.

"Ms. Collier? Hi, I'm Shirley Evans, Dr. Green's nurse. I'm sure Louise explained the office is actually closed for the day. Dr. Green is aware that you're here and will be right with you. Have a seat, if you would. Good night, Miss Collier."

Shirley could hardly keep herself from sounding as irritated as she was. The nerve of some people. *I can't believe you would actually have her come here and ask for you, Joseph Green.* The air was thick with contempt. Nancy breathed a sigh of relief as Shirley exited the clinic, locking the door behind her.

A moment later Joseph Green cautiously entered the room.

Relieved to see Shirley and Louise were gone and the office empty, he greeted Nancy.

"Hi, Sweetheart. How are you?"

"I'm okay I guess. How are you?"

"Doing fine, thanks."

Locking eyes with Nancy, he asked, "Are you okay?"

"I guess so. But obviously your two employees aren't too pleased about me showing up here."

"What do you mean? Did one of them say something out of place to you?"

"No. But they both made it clear they weren't excited about my being here."

"Well, right now they're not the ones I'm concerned about. You are. And besides, it's none of their business."

In his mind, he knew he had to keep moving ahead with his plan, not giving another thought to Shirley and Louise. He'd deal with them later. Besides, who paid their salaries? He was just glad his wife, Maggie, stayed as separate from his professional life as she did, and that their home was an hour away.

One of his biggest concerns at this moment was that Nancy was further along than what he was accustomed to dealing with himself. Being nearly twenty-four weeks, he had pressured her, knowing they were almost to the cutoff for doing this legally. Any further along and he'd be risking legal consequences for not following protocol. Granted, this one was off the record, but he was watching his back in case anything ever slipped from Nancy's mouth to someone else. To top it off, he was now faced with doing something on his own that he'd always depended on Shirley for. He took a deep breath, saying a silent prayer that nothing would go wrong.

Nancy had hidden the pregnancy from him until she simply couldn't hide it any longer. Feeling the baby moving, seeing her stomach expanding, she knew she had to tell him. His reaction had been way more emotional than expected.

"Why didn't you tell me right away?"

"I was afraid. I don't know. I knew you'd want me to get rid of it."

"Nancy, you know we've talked about waiting until after my divorce. If Maggie finds out about this, she'll have my head on a platter in court. The affair would be one thing . . . but a baby too!"

"I know, Joe. But now that it has happened, it's a whole different thing. We're not talking about what could happen here. We're talking about what has already happened. I'm pregnant with your baby!"

"Nancy, calm down. Everything is going to be okay. It'll all work out."

"Stop placating me! You don't understand, apparently, or maybe you just don't care! Have you become that calloused from all the abortions you've done? Does it not bother you that this is our child I'm feeling move inside of me?"

"Nancy, of course it bothers me." Just as he spoke the words, a wave of conviction flooded his mind—something he wasn't accustomed to feeling with all the abortions he had performed for others.

"We can have children, but we have to wait. The timing is all wrong. We need to do what we have to now. When the divorce is final, we can have all the kids you want. And we'll be able to afford them. I know this is hard, baby, but we have to do it. Trust me, it's going to all work out."

Glancing at the wheelchair in the corner, he felt a strange sense of panic. He had to get her out of here to their apartment as soon as possible. Thank goodness it was just a few blocks from the clinic. The convenience of it had served his purposes well. His wife had no idea it was home to he and Nancy. She simply thought he kept an apartment nearby for the times he was so exhausted from his shifts at the hospital. After all, the hour drive home was a long one.

"We'll leave your car here when we're done. I'll take you to the apartment and we can pick it up tomorrow."

Startled at the sound of someone entering the adjoining area, Joseph Green cautiously opened the door. Seeing the white coat, he took a breath. He forgot the courier service usually arrived at this time.

"I apologize for not letting your office know, but you'll have to come back later," he said.

"Sorry, Dr. Green. I didn't realize there was anyone still here. Apparently your girl called as she usually does at the end of the day to say you were closing early. I'll call the office and let them know we need to come back at a later time. Do you want to call us when you are ready?"

"Yes, that would be great. Thank you."

Joseph Green closed the door and took a deep breath.

"What's the matter? Is everything okay?"

"Yes, its fine, Nancy."

"What are they picking up?"

"They take care of making sure our instruments are sterile and in good order. Not a big deal. Let's just get this over with so we can both move forward."

"You know, Joe, suddenly I'm not feeling right about this whole thing. In fact, I don't feel right about anything. You keep promising we're going to be together. And yet, I don't see that happening. All I see is that you're trying to keep everything the same as it has been."

"Nancy, honey, I know you're upset. I know this is difficult for you. It will all work out for us. I promise."

"Promise me what? That suddenly your life is going to fit in with mine?"

"Nancy, please. I've got a mild sedative here I want to give you. It'll help you relax."

The inner turmoil he felt was unnerving. He turned to face

her. "Let's get this over with, sweetie. I know this is hard for you. But tomorrow will come and we'll move on. Soon it'll just be you and I and we'll be able to do whatever we want. In fact, why don't we plan to have dinner next Friday evening to discuss plans for the future?"

Not knowing how to respond, Nancy caved in emotionally. This was just one more milestone of disappointment she needed to get past. He wasn't going to step up to the plate to be her mate or a father to their child. She had listened to his lies, thinking he must love her and things would change. But instead, she had backed herself into a corner she was clamoring to escape.

Allowing Joe to give her the injection of sedative, she quickly began to feel herself relax.

When it was all over, Joseph Green placed the baby in the container. He could not do what he knew was normally done to terminate its life. The baby was fully formed at this stage. A tube would be inserted into the base of the baby's skull, and the brains were suctioned out. Frozen in fear, coming face to face with the child who was his own, he cut the umbilical cord and simply placed it in the container. He would let the service deal with the body when they returned to pick it up.

Getting this over with and getting Nancy out of the building and to their apartment was all he could think about. Physically doing harm to his own baby was more than he could bring himself to do. Once he held her in his hands, all he could do was place her aside. He cleaned up the area and Nancy in a rushed manner, and helped her get down and into the wheelchair. Closing the door behind them, he was overcome with the sense of leaving the child behind to die.

He turned his focus to Nancy, who was still groggy from the sedative.

"Let's get you home to bed, Sweetie."

Physically and emotionally offering no resistance, Nancy asked "Is it all over?"

"Yes, it's all over. Everything went fine," he consoled. Internally he was still shaken, but wasn't about to let her know that. "We'll get you to the apartment and we'll have some dinner. How about Mackin's? I'll have them prepare your favorite and deliver it!"

"I don't care. I'm not hungry. Right now I just want to get out of here." An eerie emptiness settled in. It was over. Her baby was gone. Grief swept over her like a river. She felt like she was caught up and swept away in something way bigger than herself. Something that was out of her control.

Chapter 7

Frank Burton glanced at his watch. He had gotten to work at the clinic right on time as usual. Maybe he could push a little harder tonight to see if he could get the cleaning done ahead of schedule. The news announcer interrupted the music coming through his earphones with what these days seemed a common report of disaster. He pulled the earphones off, seeking a break from the news report of a local shooting. There seemed to be so much bad news all around these days that Frank had learned to turn off as much as possible. There was no point dwelling on what he was powerless to change.

Feeling the heat from the sunlight beaming through the corridor window filled him with anticipation for the weekend. The week was just about over, and for the first time in many months the weather forecast for the weekend was good.

He had grown so accustomed to his route throughout the clinic floors, he seldom noticed the sign that had disturbed him so when he first started the job. "Restricted Entry–Clinic Personnel Only." He didn't pay attention to it like he used to.

Turning the key, he stepped in, the heaviness in the air engulfing him. It was always at this moment that something gripped him. Memories of the fear he experienced as a child when walking down dark streets popped into his mind. It was the same kind of eerie feeling of some unseen force jumping out from nowhere. Shaking it off, he put his mind on getting his scrub bucket ready to scrub the floor. *Golly, it's weird. Every time I come in this place I get the creeps.*

Looking over his shoulder, Frank reassured himself that the office was empty and everyone had already gone home as usual. He entered, knowing the sooner he finished and got out, the better.

On the rare occasions that anyone was still there, they always came off the same way. The usual stereotype he came to expect. He was the lowly janitor and they were better than him. And yet, in his heart he knew he wasn't less of a person than they. In fact in some ways he regarded himself and his family as better people. They didn't set themselves up on a pedestal. They were hardworking, respectable people.

You're a hard worker, Burton. They couldn't cope with the work you do, he mused. He wondered how they could possibly think so highly of themselves when instead of helping cure illnesses and injured bodies they were destroying life. After all, this was an abortion clinic. He silently agreed with the protesters who came from time to time to picket the clinic. He, too, believed abortions were wrong. The mystery of a new life coming into being and growing within a woman was so amazing. And there was nothing like the moment each of his kids was born. To be part of that experience as a father, in his estimation, was unparalleled. He wondered how fathers of those aborted felt about it. Considering the number of abortions he heard were taking place, he knew at least some of the fathers of these babies had to be silently struggling with what was happening to their babies.

Then he thought of all the families torn apart by divorce with kids suffering. It was all so screwed up compared to when he was growing up.

Get busy and get done, he thought. Then he thought he heard a cry.

"Frank, old buddy, you're really getting carried away now, hearing things."

Once again, the sound came. There was a baby crying, but where in the world was it? Shuddering, he heard the little voice rise again. It was coming from a lined container on a rolling tray. It wasn't the container he emptied on his route each day. Some things were out of place. He had never noticed this tray before. Then his eyes fell on what looked like a bloody mess left on a surgical chair.

Stepping over to the box on the tray, his eyes fell on the tiny body fighting to survive. Its body was moving and jerking, as though fighting to escape death. Covered with blood and waste, he saw it was a little girl. Her body was so small it barely filled his hand. Drawing her to his breast, he bolted for the door. He knew life might only be there for another moment.

Behind him, the door suddenly swung open. Frank turned to see who was entering, and the clinic doctor stepped in. Instantly he rushed toward Frank.

"What is going on here? What are you doing here?"

"I heard it cry," Frank stammered. "It's alive. My God, it's a live baby."

Joseph Green quickly stepped forward to take the infant from him.

"Oh my God, you have got to help her."

"I'll take care of this from here. Who are you?"

"I'm the janitor. Who are you?"

"I'm Joseph Green. This is my clinic. What are you doing?"
"We've got to get her over to the hospital."

"I'm so sorry, Frank, is it?" Joseph Green asked, reading Frank's name tag. "No doubt something happened I'm not aware of. I just returned from my apartment nearby to make sure everything was okay. I assure you I'll take care of it. You go ahead and . . ."

"What? Leave? Oh, no, buddy. I'm not going anywhere. We've got a live baby here and I intend to make sure she stays that way. I'm taking her over to the hospital."

"Sir, you can't do that!"

"Look, doctor! I don't know about you, but I found her and I'm taking her." With that he bolted toward the door with the tiny infant cradled in his arms.

"My name isn't 'Buddy.' It's Dr. Green, and this is my clinic you're in."

"Well, Dr. Green, I'm Frank Burton and I'm taking this baby over to the hospital."

Embracing her with the utmost care and protection, Frank Burton pushed the clinic door open and ran down the hall. The medical building was part of a complex adjoining St. Luke's Hospital. Rushing as fast as possible, he flew down the three flights of stairs to the tunnel connecting the medical building and the hospital. Feeling the baby kicking and hearing her small cry, he drew her closer.

"You're alive. My God, what kind of people are they?" Joseph Green rushed along behind.

As he swung open the door that led into the tunnel, Frank glanced ahead to the hospital entry. There were several people walking through the tunnel, some of them visitors and others staff of the hospital. The eyes of those around stared in amazement. As he approached a nurse in the tunnel, she broke stride, running to them as her eyes fell on the tiny body fighting for every breath it could take.

"Follow me," she said, glancing back at Joseph Green as she rushed into the hospital and headed for Emergency. With Frank Burton on her heels, she called the ER to alert them.

"Right in here, sir. Bring it in here. Ruth, tell George to get that life support unit from Pediatrics in here on the double."

"Hang on now, baby girl. They're gonna take care of you. Ol' Frank isn't going to leave you. I'm right here, baby."

"I'm Donna Vasquez, the Charge Nurse on duty. Are you the baby's father?"

"No."

"Well, are you a relative?"

"I'm the janitor, lady. I found her in the abortion clinic over at the medical building."

Just then Dr. Joseph Green entered. Donna's eyes widened in astonishment at what she was hearing. She was speechless.

"That's right," blurted Frank. "She was left to die. I swear that's about where these people belong."

Joseph Green motioned to the nurse to come aside. "Donna, get the baby from this guy, and get him out of the room," snarled Joseph Green under his breath.

"Mr. Burton, step out here with me, please. We will do everything we can to help her. In the meantime I need you to come with me and have a seat in the other room."

Instantly, a resistance rose up inside Frank to the nurse's suggestion. "No. I'm not going anywhere. I'm here for the duration. I found her, and I'm not leaving her. Nobody here may care what happens to her, but I do. You do what you have to. I'm not going anywhere."

"Mr. Burton, I understand you're upset, but . . ."

"I'm not leaving."

"Mr. Burton, I'm not asking you to 'leave,' I'm just suggesting it would be best for everyone if you come into the other room, try to relax a bit, and let us do what we need to do to help her."

"No. I'm not leaving, I told you that."

As another nurse entered the treatment room, the immediate need took precedence. Frank stepped back as all attention was directed to the infant. Joseph Green stepped out into the hall and dialed his cell phone.

"Greg, this is Joe Green. I'm in ER. There's a nut here with a baby he says he found in my office. I think you better get over here right away."

Nearby, Frank began to rant. "How can people do this and get away with it?"

The nurses exchanged glances, the Charge Nurse excusing herself. "I'll get Becky here to help you, Ruth," she said, closing the door. A few moments later, she reappeared.

Just then the door opened and another doctor entered. He rushed to the infant, overhearing Frank Burton's protest. He'd gotten a momentary briefing on the situation. Hearing what happened, the doctor had immediately placed a call to the hospital's executive office, reporting a very premature infant was being treated in Emergency and was reported to have been recovered in Joseph Green's Albright Clinic.

"Doctor, Mr. Burton here seems somehow concerned about leaving the baby while we are at work. I've tried reassuring him, but for some reason he is insisting on staying in the room."

The doctor glanced first at her, and then at Frank. His eyes appeared glazed over with preoccupation. "Mr. Burton, is it?"

"Yes," answered Frank.

"Mr. Burton, I'm Dr. Jonah Hanson. I am the physician

in charge at the moment. I assure you we will do everything humanly possible to see to it that this baby makes it. In the meantime, because you are not immediate family I must ask you to step outside. Given the baby's status, we will be airlifting her to Children's Hospital. They are the facility best prepared for a premature infant such as this. She'll get the best of care possible from them. I understand and appreciate your concern. Believe me, we will all do our utmost. Since you have already stated you are not related to the baby, we have to ask you to step out of the room. There are some questions we would like to ask. Why don't you go with Ruth, take a breather, and by the time you have finished the chopper should be here to transport her."

"Just know this, if she's going to Children's, I'm going to Children's. If no one else goes with her, 1 go. Make no mistake about it."

Frank didn't quite understand why, but the reassurance of this man seemed to put him at ease. The legal ramifications of such an event for the clinic hadn't entered Frank's mind, but it had almost instantly occurred to Joseph Green. He knew about the recent developments . . . how Planned Parenthood officials had been exposed, with heinous details recorded and photographed of human remains of the unborn. Any mistake such as this, if in any way associated with St. Luke's, could have devastating effects on the hospital.

Jonah Hanson knew all too well that the Executive Board of St. Luke's wouldn't take it on the chin for any physician, no matter who it was. Getting the infant and Frank Burton out of St. Luke's and as far away as possible, to Children's or anywhere else, was critical. The hospital would have no choice but to deny any involvement and let Joseph Green fall if necessary. This whole fiasco had to be headed off at the pass and he knew it.

"Mr. Burton, I can tell you are a man of great compassion. I get that. Now let us do what we can do. Go with Ruth here and take a breath."

"Okay," said Frank. "I'll take a minute. But about your questions, all I know is she was in that container in his office, left to die. Since the other containers like it were closed up, I have to believe they weren't as lucky."

After stepping into the corridor, Frank was ushered to a room by a nurse. As she opened the door, he was surprised to see it was a large plush office, evidently belonging to someone with considerable authority in the hospital.

"Have a seat, Mr. Burton. Someone will be with you in just a moment."

"Okay, but I want to call my wife," answered Frank. "By the way, I want to know right away when that air ambulance arrives. Do you hear me?" *My God, I can't believe this is happening.*

Picking up the phone to dial home, his mind went blank trying to think how he was going to explain all this to Carol. Sorrow swept over him. Knowing the compassion Carol exhibited, he found himself feeling oddly vulnerable inside. Just then, he heard a click. Little did he know just how important his concerns were to St. Luke's Hospital.

"Hi Honey."

"Oh hi, Frank. Is everything okay?"

"Yeah, I'm okay. Carol, I'm at the hospital."

"The hospital! Frank, what's wrong?"

"I'm okay, Carol. . . . It's not me. Something happened."

"What? What happened?"

"I found a baby. In the abortion clinic. I found a live baby."

"What do you mean you found a baby?"

"Yes, one live one and apparently there were also dead ones."

51

"What!"

"I went in to clean up as I always do, and I heard a baby crying. It was in a container, a plastic lined container. Her little legs and arms were going. She was crying, fighting to survive. I'm sure it was only by mistake that she was even alive."

"Oh Frank. I think I'm going to be sick."

"You! Carol, I almost passed out when I saw her. These people are crazy. And they're all trying to get me to calm down and shut up. The doctor walked in while I was there, after I found her, and tried to get me to hand her over to him. I wouldn't do it, Carol. I couldn't! I took her and ran to the hospital. All I know is that they better make sure nothing happens to her. They may have gotten the others, but they're not getting this one."

"It's a little girl?"

"Yeah. She's so tiny, you wouldn't even believe it." Just then Frank heard a knock and the door opened. In stepped Joseph Green and another man.

"Carol, someone just came in. I gotta go. I'll call you back in a little bit to let you know what's happening."

"Okay, Frank. Are you sure you're okay? I can come down there to the hospital if you want me to. Tony should be home any moment and he could watch the girls for a little while."

"No. I'm okay. They're airlifting her to Children's Hospital. I'll be going there as soon as they take off. You stay home. I'll call you back in a little while."

Frank hung up the phone and stood up.

"Mr. Burton?"

"Yeah, I'm Frank Burton."

"Mr. Burton, I'm Dr. Kyle Conrad, Chief Administrator here at St. Luke's. This is Dr. Joseph Green. I understand you reported finding a live baby. I also understand you stated it was in Dr. Green's clinic, the Albright Clinic, next door. Is that correct?"

"Yes. Only I don't think she was the only one. She just happened to be the only live one."

"Mr. Burton, I don't know what it is you think you saw, or if you did see others, but I do know we will do our best to take care of the infant you brought in."

"This is outrageous! The baby was there, alone, crying for help. I found her and in walks the doctor here who tries to get me to leave her with him and just go away. Well, I've got news for both of you, I'm not just going to go away. And no one can make me!"

"Mr. Burton, many people are opposed to abortion, and I understand that that is your right. Your personal opinions are your business. Unfortunately the issue is one that can get rather heated. The fact remains Dr. Green is practicing medicine in his clinic within the law. The choices made are those of patients and medical doctors. I don't wish to upset you any more than you already are."

"No, I bet you don't," interrupted Frank. "In fact, your staff couldn't get me out of that Emergency Room fast enough. But I'll tell you this, that little girl better make it or you're not going to hear the last of it from me. That baby was left to die. And somehow she had enough strength in her to cry for help, and I intend to see to it that she gets it."

"Mr. Burton, everyone is doing all they can to see to it that she does make it. In the meantime, I would just like to get all the facts so that we know just exactly what we're dealing with here."

"All right, mister. If facts are what you want . . . I walked into the clinic like always . . ." Turning to Joseph Green, he let go.

"Man, you're really sick, you know! You kill them and you just throw them away? Human beings. This is no different from what Hitler and his people did in Germany. You throw them in piles like garbage."

Joseph Green knew they had to get this guy settled down.

"Mr. Burton, Mr. Burton, calm down. I know you're terribly upset over what you have experienced, but we can't just accept an accusation of this magnitude without question."

"Accusation? Accusation? Who are you kidding? You know what I'm stating is fact! I found her and you walked in. Next thing I know, you'll say they aren't really people. Mister, if they aren't people, you tell me what you were when you were inside your mother and when you were born? Did you change from a mass of nothing into a human being because you came out of her body? This is insane. That argument can't even stand up in your own mind. How it has been put up with I'll never know. And why are you saying accusation? Are you trying to say she didn't come from your clinic? Is that what this is all about?"

"Mr. Burton, I don't know what you're talking about. I was on my way over here to the hospital from my clinic when you stopped me in the hall holding the baby."

Frank stood in stunned silence as he took it all in. The looks on their faces and resounding silence told it all.

"Oh . . . now I get it. This is a setup, isn't it?"

"Mr. Burton, I don't know what you're talking about. All I know is you ran up to me, holding the baby, and asking for help."

"That's a lie, and you know it! That baby was in YOUR clinic and you know that too."

"No, Mr. Burton, she was not in my clinic. I know you're upset, and we're doing everything we can to help, but the baby didn't come from my clinic."

"You're a liar!"

"Mr. Burton," Kyle Conrad continued, "why don't we take a

walk over to the medical building so you can show us just exactly what you found."

"Mr. Burton,' Kyle Conrad said, 'I think it would be best if we take a look."

"Why? Why are you so bent on going over there with me? What's the point?"

"The point is the allegations you are making need to be verified or put to rest, both for your sake as well as Dr. Green. I think a second look would be in order."

"Hey, wait a minute here, fella! He's the one who is making up stories. I go in that office every day to clean. And I went just like every other day. Only this time you hadn't cleaned up your mess before I got there."

"Mr. Burton, I'm not accusing you of anything. I'm simply stating what I know. Why don't we go over and see."

"Yeah, okay, Doc, if you insist. Let's go."

Silence rang as the three headed for the medical building.

When they reached the clinic, Joseph Green grasped the doorknob to enter. He pushed the door open and stepped inside. Holding the door for Frank and Kyle Conrad, he studied Frank's face as they entered. Frank's eyes went directly to the receptacle. When he saw the fresh bag stretched into position, he knew the others had been removed. His eyes darted at Joseph Green.

"The boxes are gone. Of course. You had everything cleaned up. I should have known. You're not stupid. You had them removed."

"Mr. Burton, my clinic is thoroughly cleaned every day." Frank headed for the door.

"You guys think you're so smart, don't you? But you know what, Doc? I don't think you're so smart at all. You're protecting yourself because you're afraid I might do something about this, aren't you?"

"Mr. Burton, all I did was attempt to help you and the baby. What I do in this clinic is perfectly legal. I have done nothing wrong."

Frank Burton stared into Joseph Green's eyes. Joseph Green nervously shifted his stance.

"Scared, Doc? I would be if I were you. You're not going to get away with this. And you know what? If anything happens to that little girl, you're never going to hear the end of it. I guarantee it."

"Are you threatening me, Mr. Burton?"

"No, Doc. I don't threaten folks."

As Frank opened the door to leave, he glanced back. Joseph Green stood immovable. Both knew this was by no means the end of the matter.

"You haven't heard the last from me!" declared Frank as he headed back to the hospital.

As the door closed, Joseph Green muttered, "Yeah, that's what I'm afraid of."

Kyle Conrad opened the door to leave and turned to Joseph Green.

"You're on your own with this one, Joe. We'll do what we can to stand behind you, but this is your own tiger to wrestle. How in the hell did you let this happen anyway?"

"I don't know what you're talking about, Kyle. Like I said, he didn't find her here."

"All right, Joe. But you know the hospital can't be tied to anything as messy as this. Not now, not ever!"

After the door closed, Joseph Green leaned up against it and covered his face. How did this happen, indeed!

Chapter 8

As the air ambulance lifted off, Frank ran to his parked truck to follow.

Hearing the chopper lift off, relieved that Frank left to follow them, Joseph Green muttered, "Holy cow. This guy is a nutcase."

Scrutinizing the office, making sure everything was cleaned up and nothing incriminating remained, he took a deep breath. The surgical tray was clean and in order. Silently he cursed himself for making mistakes. *I couldn't do it*, he thought to himself. Normally he or Shirley would have taken whatever steps were necessary to make certain the life was expired and all limbs accounted for. Because this pregnancy was as advanced as it was, and the fact that it was his own, were glaring truths he just couldn't overcome.

Continuing to think about his oversights, mistakes, and weaknesses, he thought, *I never should have had Nan come here. I should have sent her to someone else.*

To top it off, Frank Burton was going to be watching his every move along with the top dogs of St. Luke's.

57

Chapter 9

Jumping as his cell phone rang, Joseph Green breathed a sigh of relief when he saw it was Nancy calling.

"Joe?"

"Yeah, it's me."

"I need to talk."

"What is it, Nancy? Are you okay? I'm kind of got caught in the middle of an emergency here at the clinic."

Ignoring his attempt to cut her off, Nancy continued, "This has gone too far. You never intended to marry me, did you, Joe?"

"Nancy, honey, calm down. Of course I intend to. We will talk about it all, I promise."

"Our baby is gone."

"Nancy, we talked about this."

"I know we talked, but that doesn't make it right."

"Nancy, try to calm down. I know this has been very difficult for you, and it has been for me too. But sometimes we do what we have to do. We have to make decisions that are tough."

"And who is benefiting the most here, Joe? Is it me? No. I don't think so. I'm a loser, and the baby is the biggest loser of all. The only one benefiting from this situation is you. I don't believe you're concerned about my needs at all. I think this is all part of your need to cover up so you can keep going the way you always have."

"Oh, Nancy, come on. That's not true and you know it."

"Oh, do I? Not really. Ever since we met, everything has evolved around your needs and demands, not mine. Your schedule, your marriage, everything! Not once have you ever asked me what I want. Not in terms of our relationship. It's all been about you."

"Nancy, that's not true. I've tried to make you happy. Look at all I've done for you. I've taken good care of you. I've made sacrifices for you."

"Sacrifices! Is that what you call it? I call it a payoff, Joe. A bit here, and a bit there. Enough to keep me quiet so our secret relationship can continue. No, Joe. You have not sacrificed anything. And the saddest of all things is now I feel I've even sacrificed my own child. All for your advantage. All for your protection. And what do I get in return? More nights of wondering if you can get away. More frustrations at not being able to call you at home because your wife would answer."

"Nancy, you knew about my marriage right from the start. It wasn't a secret. You knew it would be like this, didn't you?"

"No, I just fell in love with you, damn it. And I still love you. But I can't keep going on like this. You either choose me or choose Maggie. No more in between."

Joseph Green thought his mind might burst if any more came at him. "I understand, Nancy. You deserve the best. And I guess I haven't been able to give it to you. I know it's been hard for you. I do love you too."

"Then love me enough to let me go."

"I'm not making you stay."

"No? Why don't you just tell me you love her more? That would at least make it easier for me to make a decision."

"Nancy, I love you very much. You've made me feel like a new man. I can't imagine life without you."

"And what about life without our baby? That's what I'm living with now. How about you?"

Hearing the click as she hung up, he drew a deep breath once again.

"What next, man? What next?"

Chapter 10

"Megan?"

No answer.

"Megan, can I come in?"

Megan faintly heard her voice, as she vacillated between sleep and consciousness.

As her mom gently shook her awake, Megan slowly opened her eyes. Time and pills had helped distance her from the events of the day. She felt despondent and subdued.

"I called the Petersons and cancelled dinner tonight. Obviously this is not a night for company. I don't know what's going on with you, but you need to let me in, Megan. As upset as you are, something tells me you're in over your head. Don't shut me out."

As she turned to leave, she bent over and kissed Megan's forehead.

"Megan, always remember what I've told you since you were just a little girl. There's nothing so bad you can't talk to us about it. Nothing! Our love for you is greater than anything you could ever do wrong. Do you hear me?"

"Yes, Mom," she replied.

"We love you, Sweetie. Now get some rest and we'll talk later."

As she heard her mother going down the stairs, Megan called her back.

Rita turned and hurried back to Megan.

"Mom, I've done something so awful!"

"What? What is it Megan?"

"Remember the day I said I was hanging out after school and came back kinda late?"

"Yes, I remember."

"Well that day Tony Burton approached me after school and asked if I would like to go to a movie and hang out with him for a while. He asked if I wanted to go by Chance's house where some of his friends were before the movie. So we went over there. Chance said his mom was home, but I never saw her. We went down to his family room where there were some other guys. Chance asked us if we wanted something to drink. We both said yes. But just a little while after he brought us the drinks he and the others left. I felt really weird, like I was drugged or something. Then Tony started coming at me, making passes. I didn't even stop him Mom! And I don't know why. It was like I couldn't make my body push him away... we had sex, Mom!"

The look on Rita Latham's face said it all. "You mean to tell me you think they drugged you?"

"Yes. But that's not all! I got pregnant. I bought a test kit at the drugstore and it was positive. Then I went to the Brewster Clinic. The doctor there confirmed I was pregnant and sent me to Albright Clinic. That's where I was today. I was at Albright Clinic having an abortion!"

Chapter 11

Ginger tate sat in her apartment, eyes closed, seeking God. She had determined within herself to spend more time in prayer, asking for guidance each day. It seemed as though the days she was true to that desire were days filled with quiet wonder. There would be times when she would see faces she hadn't seen in years. She knew it was the Lord asking her to pray for them. Then there were times when, after praying, she would feel led to call someone or go somewhere specific and wait for God to direct her to someone in need of help. She sat on the floor in utter silence. She so desired to please God.

"Lord," she whispered, "is there someone I can do something for? Show me if there is someone I can help."

She again resumed her quietness. She knew if there was someone somewhere, He was quietly waiting for her to yield herself in this way. She waited for His reply.

After a few minutes she got a strong urge to go outside. She walked down the steps of the apartment building and stepped outside. She felt the tug within to cross over to the apartment building directly opposite. Crossing the street, looking around, she saw nothing and decided to sit on the steps and wait.

After about ten minutes, a young woman approached. Ginger felt drawn to her as she climbed the stairs, holding firmly onto the rod iron rail. As the woman rang one of the units, Ginger heard her introduce herself as Amy. The buzzer sounded and she entered the building. The scent of Amy's perfume and quiet rustle of the beautiful indigo blue she wore caused Ginger to resist the sense that this beauty was the one in need. *Is she the one, Lord?*

Amy's slow and methodic movements caused Ginger to wonder if she was in physical pain. As Amy disappeared within the building Ginger continued to pray. "Show me if she's the one, Holy Spirit. Thank You for Your direction."

Sitting on the steps under the bright starlit sky, Ginger drank in the tranquility that so permeated her spirit. She was daily struck with thankfulness for her new life. Whenever she pondered days gone by, she never failed to be in awe of how changed she was. The narrow escapes from death's door, even before she knew Him, were so incredible. She sometimes wondered who prayed for her. Somewhere along the line she knew someone had. There had been too many close calls. And it wasn't as though she turned to the Lord with her first dark encounter. His faithfulness had extended over many years while she just walked in rebellion to all that was good.

Hearing the music seeping through the door into the hall let Amy know Jim was probably in the middle of getting high with friends. After knocking, she heard him approach the door. When he looked through the peephole and saw Amy, he opened the door with a huge smile. His eyes and slow speech told the story. He was stoned and had company.

"Hey, Amy! How ya doin', baby? You're looking beautiful as ever. And smellin' good too. Come on in. A couple of my friends are here I'd like you to meet."

He was already heading down the hall toward the living room. Amy followed, disdaining the moment. She had no interest in meeting anyone at that moment. New faces or familiar, she wasn't interested. They were all part of a life she no longer wanted any part of. She simply wanted to get her pills and be gone. The overpowering smell of the dope was second only to the cloud of smoke in the room.

After saying hello to the friends Jim introduced her to, she quietly turned to him and explained she was in a bit of a rush and couldn't stay.

"Did you get those things I called you about?" she asked, using the proper protocol of masked communication.

"Oh, yeah, yeah. C'mon in the kitchen."

Once there, the communication, which was normally warm and friendly with Jim somehow, was intensely hollow tonight.

After exchanging the pills and cash, Amy turned to go.

"Thanks, Jim."

"Yeah, sure, Amy. Are you okay?"

"Yeah, I'm okay."

"You seem kind of different."

"Oh, well, I'm a little under the weather, I guess. But I'll be okay now," she said, grinning and holding up the package of pills he just sold her.

Jim grinned, assuming he knew what the inference was. As Amy turned to go she suddenly was aware of the distance between them. They were oceans apart. It was as if she barely knew this guy. The vulnerability of his position as a drug dealer always was in the foreground of their exchanges. He knew all too well that at any moment any of his "patrons" could suddenly turn "informer" or even become a setup for a rip-off.

Once outside the apartment, starting down the hall, Amy was aware of her aloneness. All attempts on her part to align herself with people ended this way . . . oceans apart. It was what had become normal. The strength to continue enduring wasn't there. She knew that the well inside had finally run dry. The strength to continue no longer existed. The void of determination within spoke loudly of the end she had found.

Her despondency was surprising even to her. She honestly no longer cared. She didn't want this to be a passing thing; she wanted to see an end to it all. As she passed a mirror in the foyer of the apartment building, she was struck with the beauty of all that adorned her and the hope of death that it enshrouded. Stepping out into the night air, the freshness of the evening breeze brushed her. She saw the same woman she'd seen earlier still sitting on the steps, and quickly moved to the side to pass by.

$\approx$

As the door opened and Amy stepped out, Ginger knew from the urgency within her that this was the person she had been sent to.

As Amy reached the bottom stair, Ginger blurted out, "Excuse me, Miss."

Amy started not to respond, but something inside wouldn't allow her to refuse. She turned and looked at Ginger.

"Yes," she answered.

Ginger's heart was overrun with a love and compassion she had come to recognize as the Lord's. She experienced it at times like this when she stepped out in obedience to Him and got in touch with the pain of others. Looking into Amy's eyes, she saw the pit of hopelessness and despair the enemy had dug.

"I know this may sound really strange, but do you need help?" As she continued to peer into Amy's gaze, there was no answer. She continued. "Do you know the Lord?"

The look of surprise emanating from Amy's once blank gaze confirmed she was reaching out to the right person. Continuing, Ginger said, "I . . . I was praying. I live right across the street there, and I felt such a strong urgency to come here. That someone really needed help. Do you? Do you need help?"

Amy stood, paralyzed with the realization of what was happening. Her mind filled with a clear recollection of what she had said just a couple of hours before. She heard the silent cry within. *Oh, God. You really are there.*

"Do you know the Lord? Do you know Jesus?"

As Amy's eyes filled with tears, she was totally speechless with what was taking place.

"He loves you. Do you know that? He wants to help you. Do you know that?"

Amy placed her hand over her mouth as the sobs began to break forth. She could only shake her head in acknowledgment.

Ginger stood up and approached her. Unlike the stiff response to her first words, Amy's resistance was totally washed away in that moment. Putting her arms around Amy, Ginger held her close. The two rocked with the emotion. The utter despair and grief that swept through Ginger at that moment was a meshing together of the two lives. She became totally enveloped in all the pain Amy had within. And then she began to pray.

"Help, Holy Spirit. Oh help her, Lord. You know, Lord. I don't. You know what she needs. Oh, Jesus."

At the mention of that name, the sweetest presence and release Amy had ever experienced was all that was present. She knew. He was here. In this woman. He was real and He was alive. It was true all along. *It's true*, thought Amy. *He's real and He really, really loves me.*

The two locked eyes and there was a breakthrough. In place of the pit of despair, there was a river of hope breaking through.

Ginger continued to hold her, totally engulfed in God's presence.

"What's your name?" Ginger asked.

"Amy."

"Amy, I'm Ginger. I live right across the street here. Come home with me. Let's go to my apartment and talk."

Never before had an invitation been so welcome. Amy simply nodded her head. Ginger put her arm around Amy's waist, hugging her. This was someone really special she wanted to know.

As they sat talking, Amy knew she had finally found what was real. A reality that was somehow definable. It wasn't the fleeting notion of figuring things out while going through the maze of life's experiences. What, up until now, had been a ridiculous fairy tale people chose to use to cope with life now revealed itself as the underlying answer to so many of life's questions.

Jesus was really real. Now she grasped the reality of the peace she saw in that teacher's face. It was the same peace she saw in Ginger. Amy was amazed as Ginger shared the life of drugs and rebellion she had come out of. The stereotype she had always applied to "Christians" was quickly being exposed for the lie it was. This dynamic woman was so full of life and love. True, heartfelt love.

For hours they shared. Amy had never before been able to

expose herself to another without fear of rejection and judgment, or simply being taken advantage of. But this woman was so free, and as Amy shared the fragmented parts of her life, she felt herself breaking away and letting go of the torment and despair she had known as life up until now.

"Whatever has happened, whatever you have done, Amy, He forgives you. That is why He died for us."

When Ginger asked what had happened that day, Amy found it extremely difficult to speak of the baby. It wasn't a fear of judgment, but purely a remorse that coursed deep within. The shame once again began to overtake her. As she forced herself to share about it, Ginger looked on with understanding.

"I know, Amy," she responded. She peered deep within her eyes and quietly said it again. "I had an abortion too."

Somehow that confession carried more relief with it than all those they shared. This woman, so filled with the love of God, identifying God as her personal friend, had done the very thing that had nearly caused Amy to end her life.

Being well acquainted with the guilt that abortion had brought, Ginger was able to speak into those most vulnerable thoughts and feelings. "Our babies are with the Lord, Amy. They don't feel pain anymore. They don't even remember what they went through. God doesn't allow those things to remain with us when we go on to be with Him. We can't change it, Amy. We can only receive His forgiveness and ask Him to heal the memory."

Suddenly Amy's mind was filled with thoughts of her baby, alive and happy. The pictures of death and torment were being replaced with an awareness of life she never knew existed. Life in an entirely separate realm. "Does that mean we'll get to see them again?" asked Amy.

"Oh yes, I definitely believe we will. I don't think there is any question about it. In fact, I've often thought about my baby, and what it's going to be like to see him or her for the first time. I believe it's the same for them as it is for the babies that are miscarried, or anyone else who dies."

The thought of her baby being alive flooded Amy's heart. To think she would someday see, touch, and hold it close . . . but what if the baby didn't want her? What if it just didn't even want to know her?

Ginger broke the silence with a thought she knew was prompted by the Lord. "It's okay, Amy. The guilt is there, I know. But God will help you deal with it. It's not anything anyone else can do for you. Only God and time will lessen the pain. There are some things we just have to go through. Forgiving ourselves is always one of the hardest parts. That's exactly what the enemy doesn't want you to do. As long as he can keep you hung up on your past mistakes, he will. Ask the Lord to help you. He will. I'll help you. We can study the Bible together and pray. I'll be here for you. I promise. Believe me; the Bible and prayer are what will get you through. It's the book with all the answers."

Amy sat amazed. Just yesterday if someone had told her this, she would have laughed and called it hysterical nonsense. Pray and read the Bible? Jesus? What a fool she had been. What just hours before was hysterical nonsense had suddenly become the answer to it all. In place of despair and confusion about the future, she saw a way to live with hope.

"Oh, Jesus," was all she could say.

Chapter 12

Tony shook his head as he recalled the last three weeks. As cool as he tried to appear to everyone, the pressure within had been intense. He was back and forth between what Megan had just told him and what her parents would say. He thought back to the night he and Megan had sex. The struggle to restrain himself physically was impossible . . . besides, everybody was doing this. He wondered why he felt ashamed. His friends never seemed to question any of it. Sure, he felt like a jerk when he backed off from Megan. He didn't like Megan thinking he didn't care but he was in way over his head and he knew it. Maybe no one else would find out. Maybe Megan would just keep it secret.

Stepping into the kitchen, his head dropped when his eyes met his mother's.

"Hi, honey. I'm glad you're home. Where have you been?"

"Sorry I'm late, Mom. I ran into some of the guys after school and we shot a few hoops at the park."

"You won't believe what happened to your father today. He called about a half hour ago and said he was at the hospital."

"The hospital! What's wrong?"

"Nothing's wrong with him. He found a live baby in one of

the offices he cleans. It's an abortion clinic. He said he heard it crying. He said there were some cartons in the clinic that he'd never noticed before, and that one was open and this tiny, tiny baby was inside of it. Oh, Tony. The thought of all those little babies. And then to think one even lived through it and was just left behind for dead. I can't even imagine what your father must be going through."

Silent with shock, Tony wondered, *Megan was at the clinic today. Could the baby Dad found be theirs?*

Hearing Frank's truck pulling to a stop in the back yard, Carol turned from Tony, stepping out of the house to embrace her husband. When their eyes met, the pain and anger Carol saw was overwhelming. She knew this man better than anyone else and yet what she saw in him was way beyond any normal upset.

"How's the baby?" she stammered.

"So far, so good—so they say. The question is, can we believe them? They already let me know they'll deny it was from the clinic."

"But how can they? You were right there!"

"Before I left to follow the helicopter to Children's, a doctor from the hospital took me back to the clinic. It had all been cleaned up and the clinic doctor said for all he knows the baby was from somewhere else. He's not going to admit it, even though he knows I'm telling the truth. I'm telling you, Carol, nothing makes sense anymore. They're killing babies and they call it abortion. They say it's a 'choice.' But who ever asked the babies? They're tearing them apart. They're ripping their little bodies to shreds, and they say it's their right! They're sadistic barbarians. Killing babies as though they don't really exist. Their bodies are right there. They have to look at them and plainly see. Those babies are people. They're as real as you and me. Anyway, she's in what they call the neonatal ICU at the hospital. No doubt I'll have to go over there later to find out what's happening. They won't tell me because I'm not 'family.' Ain't that a kicker! I'm the only one in the world she has. Whatever 'family' she had killed her."

Listening from the dining room, the words his father spoke exploded in Tony's thoughts. He knew for sure he couldn't bear to hear any more. If his dad ever found out it could destroy their relationship. This was the first time he found himself on the side of what his dad identified as an opponent, but it wasn't because he had chosen to be there. He turned to leave. Slipping out the front door, the door slammed behind him. There was no way he could face him at this moment.

Hearing the door slam, Carol called out, "Tony." When she heard no reply, she turned back to Frank.

"I wonder where he's going. Why do you suppose he left?"

"Did he hear me tell you what happened at the clinic today?" asked Frank.

"Yes. He just got home a few minutes ago, and I told him what happened just before you drove up. I'm sure he heard you talking just now. He didn't say anything about going anywhere. Do you think he's just upset over what happened?"

"I don't know, Carol. Right now I don't know if I can even think about what's going through his mind. I just hope what we've taught these kids has sunk in, because there sure is enough out there to screw 'em up. Maybe it's good for him to hear about what's really going on out there. Somebody better tell them, or they'll never know."

The phone rang. Frank's mind immediately went to the baby girl back at the hospital. He breathed a sigh of relief when he heard Carol's response, acknowledging the call was for her. What came as a welcome relief quickly vanished, though, as he watched Carol's facial expression change and heard the concern in her voice. As she hung the phone up the look on her face told Frank something was wrong.

"What is it, Carol? What's wrong now?"

"That was Rita Latham. Megan's mother."

When Frank showed no sign of recognition Carol continued.

"I guess Tony and Megan have been spending time together lately. She said something has happened that she and her husband need to talk to us about. She sounded as though it was pretty serious. I told her we were in the middle of dealing with something and tonight wasn't the best for us, but she insisted. They want to stop over in about an hour."

"What in the world is that all about?" asked Frank.

"I have no idea. I hope Tony isn't in some kind of trouble. He's been pretty skittish the last few weeks. I didn't think too much of it. Teenagers with all their moods. You never know what's causing their attitude to change."

"He better not be in trouble with their daughter. That's the last thing we need to deal with now."

Chapter 13

There was a small coffee shop where kids from school hung out. When Tony approached it, he was actually relieved none of them were there. Slipping into a booth, dialing Megan's number, he took a deep breath, not knowing what to say if she answered.

"Hi, Megan. It's Tony. I just wanted to see if you're okay."

She responded with silence.

"I'm sorry I've been such a jerk, Megan. I guess I got scared after what happened and didn't know what to do."

"What do you have to be scared about? You're not the one who got pregnant."

"I know. I totally get that. Megan, I don't know how to tell you this but something really bizarre happened to my dad today."

"What?"

"Well, he works as a janitor at the Albright Clinic and today he was cleaning the abortion clinic office and there was a live baby in a container he found."

"What are you talking about, Tony?"

"He found a live baby."

"You have got to be kidding!"

"No, I'm not kidding. He picked it up and ran next door to the hospital."

"It can't be ours, Tony. I was less than two months along."

"Well, thank God for that, but it doesn't change the fact that he found what he did."

"That's just great. And now my parents are on their way to your house to talk about what happened with us. I cannot handle any of this anymore. I had to tell them. They know about what happened at Chance's, they know I was pregnant, and they know I went and had an abortion today."

Chapter 14

Carol and Frank felt the tension being projected by the Latham's as they all took a seat in the living room.

Rita glanced over at Larry as she nervously began. "Today Megan came home from school early. I knew something was wrong. She said she didn't feel well. But I had no idea just how bad it was. After she went up to her room for a while, I went to check on her.' Larry placed his arm around her on the couch to comfort her. 'What she told me was totally devastating, both to Megan, but also to us. Apparently she and Tony had sex about two months ago at Chance Morgan's house after school one day. Megan said she thinks she may have been drugged."

"Oh dear God, no!" whispered Carol.

Frank silently let the news sink in. "Are you kidding me? But, how do we know for sure it was Tony?"

"Mr. Burton, I know this must be hard for you and Mrs. Burton as well. But Megan wasn't lying. I know my daughter. She would never accuse Tony if he weren't the one. She also said she doesn't know who it was that drugged her. She said it might have been Chance since he was the one that gave them drinks. The problem is, it doesn't end there. It turns out Megan got pregnant and went for an abortion today at Albright Clinic. That's why she seemed so sick when she got home."

Frank's mind flooded with the gruesome reality of finding the baby abandoned to die at the clinic. And now one of the babies aborted was Tony's. Their own grandchild.

Larry Latham spoke up. "We're not here to attack Tony, but we've got to hold these kids accountable for what they've done. We had to come to you with this. They've got to understand the magnitude of what has taken place. We've also got to find out if someone slipped her something when they were at Chance's house. Maybe it was Tony. Maybe it was someone else, but we need to find out. This has got to be exposed and dealt with."

Carol hesitated, not knowing what to say. "I agree. We've got to find out. I can't even imagine Tony doing such a thing. I know Chance's parents don't keep as close of an eye on him as we would like. I didn't know Tony was hanging out at his house. He's talked about him before, but it sounded like it was other guys from the team that were hanging out there, and Tony thought Chance was kind of a bully and jerk."

"Frank and I will talk to Tony about this," Carol said. "Because of what you're telling us, I think it might be best to talk to him alone at first. He might be more willing to open up and tell us what exactly happened."

Larry rose from the couch. "Carol and Frank, can we call you by your first names?"

"Of course," responded Carol.

"Rita and I are extremely upset. Our daughter is devastated, and it sounds like something very underhanded has taken place. I try to not jump to conclusions too fast. I know from experience there's always more to the story than you think. But, obviously we feel Tony has to be held accountable for his part in this.

Megan didn't seem to think he would intentionally slip something in a drink, but she wasn't as sure sounding about Chance. Whether Tony or Chance did though, we need to find out and put a stop to it before other girls get hurt."

"Oh, you can be sure we'll find out," said Frank. "And when we do, we will be getting in touch with you."

Carol looked over at Frank. "I think we need to explain what happened at your work today to the Latham's. It's too much of a coincidence not to."

After hearing what had taken place at the clinic, Rita and Larry Latham both sat in silent astonishment.

After a few long moments, Rita broke the silence. "The baby you found was alive? Is it still alive?"

Frank responded, "She's at Children's Hospital. When I left the hospital, she was still alive."

Rita shrieked, "Oh, Lord, what if she's ours?"

"I don't think that's possible.' Carol said. "Megan wasn't far enough along for it to be the same baby. The one Frank found was around half-term already."

"What's going to happen to her?" asked Rita.

"I don't know," Frank replied, shaking his head. "That's what I have to find out."

Chapter 15

Watching the Lathams drive away, Carol closed the door and turned to Frank. "What are we going to do?"

"I'm going to find Tony and get to the bottom of this. No wonder he's been so skittish."

"Frank, wait. You need to calm down before going anywhere. Tony must be scared to death."

"You know, Carol, I'm sure he is scared out of his wits. I would be too if I were him. But scared or not, he's going to have to answer some pretty tough questions. After what I saw today he has got to understand his own child and our grandchild is dead because of what he and Megan did."

Turning to leave, Frank gave Carol a kiss on the forehead.

"Stay here, Carol. If he shows up, don't let him out of your sight."

In an attempt to soften the confrontation between Frank and Tony, Carol said, "Remember, Frank, Tony's just a kid. He didn't know that it was going to end up like this."

As he quickly went down the back steps to the garage, Carol shuddered. "Oh, God, don't let anything worse happen. Please, Father, protect Tony and Frank."

Frank pulled up in front of the coffee shop, spotted Tony in a booth, and rolled down the passenger-side window.

Seeing his dad's truck pull up and motion for him to come out, Tony knew there was no avoiding this.

Climbing in the truck, he said. "Hi, Dad. Is everything okay?"

"Megan Latham's parents just left the house. They came over to tell us some pretty shocking news."

Trying to act dumb, Tony responded weakly. "Really? What did they say?"

"You know perfectly well what they came to see us about, don't you?"

Tony blankly stared at Frank. "I don't know what to say, Dad. I didn't know anything about it until today. Megan told me afterward what she had done."

"Is that what this was? Something Megan did? And what about you? What did you do? And what about the baby? Really, Tony! That baby belonged to our family too."

As his father pulled away from the curb, the anger and frustration Tony saw in his dad was so extreme he just shut him mouth and sat tight. When they headed in a direction away from home, Tony asked, "Where are we going?"

"We're going to take a ride to Albright Clinic. I want you to see where I found that baby girl today. And then we're going to the hospital to see what's happening."

Pulling up near the entry of the clinic, Frank parked the truck. Tony nervously looked around. Glancing up to the windows of the clinic he knew so well, Frank saw the lights were on. Frank jumped up into the truck bed, unlocked his tool case, and pulled out his shotgun.

"Dad! What are you doing with a shotgun?"

"There's someone I want you to meet. Maybe I can give him a little perspective on his own life, since he doesn't seem to care about others. Come with me, son."

"Dad, what are we doing here?" Entering the building, terror overcame Tony.

Frank got on the elevator and pushed the third-floor button, standing in silence, ignoring Tony's questions. Being past hours, Albright Clinic was closed.

"Dad, please! You can't go threaten someone with a shotgun!" Tony cried in desperation.

Exiting the elevator, Frank held the door for Tony to follow. Frank turned the key to unlock the clinic door, and they both stepped inside. Joseph Green looked up from his desk, scotch bottle and glass in hand. Seeing Frank Burton, shotgun in hand, the numbing effect of alcohol suddenly vanished.

"Hey, Tony, this is the man I wanted you to meet. This is Dr. Joseph Green. He's the one who runs this clinic. He's the one who performs all the abortions here."

Joseph Green stood perfectly still, knowing a wrong move could potentially cost him his life. He looked at Tony and wondered who this frightened teenager was with Frank Burton.

"Dr. Green, this is my son, Tony."

Joseph Green acknowledged Tony with a nod. "How do you do."

Tony stared blankly in return.

"Tony, why don't you tell Dr. Green what happened today."

He hung his head and softly said. "My girlfriend came here for an abortion today."

"That's right, Doc. Hear that? You killed my grandchild today."

Joseph Green froze with terror. One wrong move and Frank Burton could blow him to bits.

"Dad," Tony pleaded, "please don't do this."

"I think someone should make sure this man doesn't kill any more babies, don't you, Tony?"

"Dad, you can't kill this man. Even if you did, it wouldn't do any good. There are doctors everywhere that do abortions."

"What do you do with the babies you kill, Doc?"

"You mean fetuses?

"No, I mean the babies."

"Actually, the remains are carefully removed and sent to a special facility. Important research is done with them."

"You're telling me you use them for experiments?"

"No, I don't do anything with them. I don't really know exactly what happens after they are removed, but I have been reassured the remains are treated with utmost respect and care and sometimes there are procedures that they are part of that help the greater good."

Frank's steel stare into Joseph Green's eyes made it clear. This wasn't someone Joseph Green could just reason everything away with.

"Mr. Burton," he nervously continued, "my practice provides services to women. For a variety of reasons, many of them find they are not suited for motherhood and sometimes, because of health concerns for the mother or baby, an unreasonable risk is posed by pregnancy."

"What about the risk to those babies? You killed my grandchild, Doc. You know that, don't you? And my kid, my own son went along with all the lies you guys tell them. All that matters is what covers your own tracks. Isn't that right? Isn't that the gauge you use? You make big money, and they're silent through the whole thing. The women don't say a thing because it gets them out of a tight spot, and the babies can't say anything. That's a pretty sad state of affairs, don't you think?"

Tony hung his head in shame. He knew his father was right. He knew in his heart this man, whom he so admired, stood up for what he believed in and what he believed was right. The tears streamed as he saw the lines clearly drawn. He knew he had chosen the wrong side, and he knew he was being called back into line with what was right.

Frank shifted the shotgun in his hands. "I could shoot you right now for killing my own flesh and blood. But you're not worth it. I'm not going to jail for that and tearing my family apart. And I'm not going to stoop to your level."

Joseph Green and Tony both breathed sighs of relief.

"C'mon, Tony. Let's get out of here."

Watching Frank and Tony disappear down the hall, Joseph Green closed the door to his clinic, sobbing with relief. How had things gotten so out of control? These right-wing nuts were crazy. He wasn't breaking any law. As he held with tenacity to his own defense, his conscience raged against the reasoning.

Chapter 16

Larry Latham spotted Frank's truck in the clinic's lot, and pulled to a stop alongside it. Carol had been right when she'd told him she was afraid Frank might be out to go after Joseph Green.

Unaware of the prayers Carol continued to pour out, Frank found his rage had completely defused. He hadn't really contemplated shooting Joseph Green. He just wanted to see his face at the threat of death.

Larry breathed a sigh of enormous relief when the door to Albright Clinic had opened and Tony and Frank emerged. He hadn't heard any gunshots. They were walking and not running. That was a good sign. Carol had been right about how serious this man could be. Larry swallowed hard as he got out and approached Frank and Tony.

Frank strained against the glare of the lights overhead. "What the heck is he doing here?"

Tony stiffened.

"What are you doing here?" demanded Frank.

"Carol called us. She was worried," Larry explained. He didn't mention the fact that she told him the shotgun was missing.

"How'd you know I'd be here?"

"I didn't. Just a wild guess. What can I do to help?"

"Nothing unless you can bring our baby back."

"Unfortunately none of us can do that, Frank."

"Yeah, I bet the old doc wishes he could."

"Is he up there?" asked Larry.

"Yeah. He's up in his office. Tony and I just paid him a visit."
Tony hung his head, nervously looking around.

"What happened?"

"Much of nothing, really. He went on and on about how he was doing a 'good service' to these women who are in trouble. But then he's got to come up with a reason for all the bucks he's making."

"You know he can't really understand what he's doing, don't you?' asked Larry. 'The guy's obviously bought the lie—hook, line, and sinker—just like so many others."

Frank glared at him. "What are you talking about? The guy knows what he's doing, and he doesn't care. He killed our grandchild today and gave it to science for experimentation. How do you handle the babies and not know what you're doing?"

"People do all kinds of things for money and security. It's not so much what they're doing, as it is how deceived they are."

"Hey, wait a minute. Whose side are you on, anyway? This guy is making a business out of killing babies."

"What he's doing is wrong, completely wrong. And what Megan and Tony did is wrong. But I don't think he really realizes what he is doing."

"I don't buy it. The kids, yes. But not him. This guy is doing this every day. I guess that's where we differ. I call a spade a spade. This man is a killer, and he's getting paid to do it. And I don't intend to stand by and let him keep doing it without saying something about it."

"Frank, I think you're right. I don't think we should be quiet about it. I think we can really make a difference, if we handle this the right way."

"Okay, so what do you suggest we do?"

"Well, first we hope and pray that the little girl makes it. Then we make sure what took place is made known."

"Somehow or another this guy has got to pay. The hospital is already backing him up. In front of me he told them a boldfaced lie that the baby didn't come from his clinic. That he 'ran into me' in the hall of the clinic building as I was running for help."

"I'll stand with you, Joe. And I'll stand with Tony, as long as I know he didn't drug Megan."

Tony did an about-face. "Drug Megan? No way! Mr. Latham, if anything, Chance drugged both of us. I didn't find out until days later that Megan felt she had been given something. I was feeling kind of the same way. Only what they gave me made me more aggressive . . . if you know what I mean?" Blushing, Tony recalled the surge of sexual aggressiveness that overcame his body that day.

"Tony," Larry Latham continued, "if that is the case and both you and Megan were drugged, we need to get to the bottom of that as well."

Turning to Frank, he continued. "Sounds like you and I have more than one guy to deal with. If Chance did what we think he did, then there's something major there we've got to address as well. I'll contact Chance's parents. We'll start there. In the meantime, if you can keep us informed as to what's happening with the baby, and with this Dr. Green, we'll lend all the help and support we can."

"That's fine. Tony and Carol and I are available to meet with you and Chance's family as well. In the meantime, I've got a baby at Children's Hospital I've got to check on."

"All right, Tony, let's go see how our girl is doing."

Chapter 17

The ride to Children's Hospital was an eternity for Tony. The receptionist looked up in surprise when he and Frank arrived entered.

"We're on our way up to the neonatal ICU," Frank said.

"Sir, I'm sorry, but it's well past visiting hours."

"Well, it may be well past visiting hours, but this isn't just a visit. I'm Frank Burton. There was a baby airlifted here earlier today. I'm here to see how she is doing?"

"Sorry sir, but as I said, it's past visiting hours."

"C'mon, Tony." As they headed toward the elevators the receptionist dialed security.

"There is a man and his son headed to the elevators. He said something about a baby being airlifted in today to neonatal ICU. I saw a memo earlier giving us a heads-up to watch for him. I tried to stop him, but he's not listening."

Exiting on the second floor, Frank was determined to find her. "My name is Frank Burton. A newborn was airlifted over from St. Luke's today. Is this the floor she's on?"

"Are you a member of the family?"

"That's the million-dollar question. Nobody knows who her family is. I found her in an abortion clinic today over at Albright Clinic. I'm the one person who wants her alive. Is this the floor she's on?"

Just then the security guard approached. He was an elderly fellow with a gentle manner. "Sir, can we help you?"

"Here we go again! Look, I just explained to this nurse. I'm looking for a baby that was airlifted in here today. I just want to know where she is and how she's doing."

The nurse stood. "It' okay, Al. I'll handle this. The baby is in Isolation so no one can see her except immediate family.

Please have a seat and I'll see if I can find anything out for you."

Tony gingerly pulled his dad's arm to get him to back off and sit down. Meanwhile, the station nurse was on the phone attempting to get instructions on what to do. She too had been told about the baby transferred from St. Luke's and was forewarned a man might show up. She hung up the phone and spoke softly and assuredly to Frank.

"Mr. Burton, the baby is being given the best care available. We are doing everything possible. Because you are not a family member, I cannot release information or let you see her. I'm sorry."

"Is she going to make it?" Frank asked.

"Mr. Burton, I'm sorry. There is nothing more I can tell you." Tony peered at her in silent wonder.

Joseph Green walked in. He stopped in his tracks when he saw Frank and Tony.

Frank glared at him. "Well, look who's here." What Frank Burton failed to understand was that Joseph Green was there to check on his own child.

When Joseph Green failed to respond to Frank, Frank turned away in disgust. "Time to go, son." Turning to Joseph Green, he said, "Make sure she's well cared for, Doc. I'll be back."

Fighting to maintain his own reputation and authority, Joseph Green looked at the charge nurse. He would not let this man destroy all that he had worked so hard to build.

"I'm Dr. Joseph Green from St. Luke's. I'm here to check on the patient that was admitted today."

The nurse watched Frank and Tony Burton get on the elevator to leave. "Right this way, Dr. Green."

Entering the room, Joseph Green was overcome with compassion. The tiny life before him was his own daughter. He never would have imagined her being here, fighting for her life.

Chapter 18

Hanging the phone up, Carol took a deep breath. Larry's call put her worst fears to rest. Joseph Green had not fully incurred the rage she knew Frank was feeling toward Joseph Green.

"C'mon, Frank. Bring Tony and come home," she pleaded out loud, peeking through the kitchen curtains.

Minutes passed and she began to question what Frank might have done after leaving the clinic building. Thoughts ran rampant. She paced the floor, praying. "Oh Lord. Bring them home, please. Father, speak to Frank. Give him understanding and wisdom with Tony. Speak to Tony too. Help them, Lord."

Opening her Bible, her source of constant stability, sanity, and hope, she read, "The time for repentance is speeding by like chaff whirled before the wind! Therefore consider, before God's decree brings forth the curse upon you, before the time to repent is gone like the drifting chaff, before the fierce anger of the Lord comes upon you—yes, before the day of the wrath of the Lord comes upon you!"

"Oh, Lord, open our eyes. Let us see the evil of our ways."

She closed her eyes as the tears streamed down. How often she had prayed for Frank to see the truth.

She lurched as the phone rang. "Hello?"

"Carol, its Brad Johnson, Frank's supervisor. I'm sorry to be calling so late, but I need to speak to Frank."

"He's not here, Brad. Is something wrong?"

"Carol, I just got a call from George Thompson. . . . Apparently he got a call from our CEO about an incident at work today. He's been asked to remove Frank and reassign him elsewhere."

"What? I don't believe this," Carol replied.

"Carol, I know this is a shock, and you know how I feel about Frank. He's the best we have. Only, they want him moved. There's really nothing I can do about it."

"I don't believe it."

"Carol, do you know when Frank will be back?"

"I don't know. I would hope any moment."

"Well, could you have him call me?"

"Yeah, sure, Brad. But, where are you assigning him then?"

"That's just it, Carol. I don't have another place to put him right now on such short notice. I'll have to see what I can do about switching out someone else."

"How much did George tell you, Brad?"

"He really didn't tell me anything. All I know is they don't want Frank back at the clinic."

"No, I'll bet they don't!"

"What do you mean, Carol?"

"I think I better wait and let Frank tell you about it, Brad."

"All right. Ask him to call me tonight if it's not too late when he gets home. Otherwise, just have him call me in the morning."

Carol put the receiver down and shook her head in disbelief.

"How can they do this? They don't want him back there. Oh, this is too crazy. Fourteen years he's been there. Fourteen years!"

When she heard the truck pull up to the garage, she breathed a sigh of relief. She ran to the door to greet them, and looked directly into Frank's eyes to get a read on where things were at between him and Tony. Tony sheepishly slipped behind Frank's back to avoid her. Tony hadn't seen her since taking off earlier that day with the news of the baby. He couldn't bring himself to look at her directly.

Carol asked Frank, "Is everything all right?"

"Yeah, we're okay."

Carol turned to Tony. She went over and put her arms around him. He pulled back, feeling completely ashamed of himself.

His mother always made it clear how highly she thought of him. "Where did you go?" she asked Frank.

"We were at the clinic, as you probably well know. I'm sure your buddy, Larry Latham, called to let you know."

"Yes, I know you were at the clinic, Frank. But where did you go from there?"

"We went up to the hospital to check on the baby."

"How is she?"

"All right as far as I know. But they aren't going to tell me anything. I don't trust any of them."

Carol looked at Tony. Suddenly she saw him in a different light. He wasn't her little boy anymore. "Tony, why don't you go take a shower and get ready for bed? I want to talk with your father."

This was the moment of escape he was hoping for. "Sure, Mom." Turning to go, he looked back. "I'm really sorry, Mom! I didn't mean for any of this to happen."

"Okay, well we'll talk more. Go get a shower. As he walked away she said, "I love you, Tony."

"Yeah, I know. I love you, too, Mom."

As she poured Frank a cup of hot coffee, Carol knew this night wasn't anywhere near over.

"They're nuts. You know that, Carol?"

"Yes, I know, Frank. Just about everything in this world is nuts."

"Do you know that bastard actually told us he was 'doing these women a service'? Can you believe that? And then Larry Latham comes along and says he doesn't realize what he's doing. I mean, my God. The man is doing these operations himself. How could he not know what he's doing?"

"Frank, I don't think Larry meant he doesn't know what he's doing. They've got to be in complete denial. Like somehow detaching themselves. Otherwise they wouldn't be able to do it. It's like an evil power has clouded their thinking and made them believe there's no afterlife. That they won't be accountable to God for what they've done."

"Well, he may not have before. But if that's the case, he will by the time I get through with him."

"Frank . . . there's something more I need to tell you." Her tone of voice caused him to stop and look in her eyes.

"What?"

"Brad Johnson called."

"From work?"

"Yes."

"And . . . ?"

"He said he got a call from George Thompson, and you're being assigned to a different building."

"What?"

"You're not supposed to go back to work at the medical building. He said you are being assigned to another site. He doesn't know where yet. It'll take a day or so to get it figured out."

"All right. That's it! I've had all I'm going to take of this."

"What do you mean?"

"Don't you get it, Carol? The clinic pays them for our service. Since I found what I did today, and tried to get help for that baby, they will do all they can to keep me as far away as possible. Joseph Green is probably threatening to pull his business if they don't get me out of there. Well, I've got news for them! They're not getting rid of me that easy. I promised that baby I'd be there for her, and they aren't going to stop me."

"But, what about your job, Frank?"

"What about it, Carol? I'm going to do what I have to do.

And I will not let Joseph Green, George Thompson, or anybody else stop me. If they're going to fight, then I'll fight back."

"Frank, you've got to calm down. I know you're doing what you believe is right, but don't let them push you into doing something you'll regret. Larry Latham told me that you had your shotgun with you and that you confronted Joseph Green. Don't you understand what they can do to you?"

"Carol, I'll be fine. If I have to go get a job somewhere else, that's what I'll do. But they're not gonna get rid of me this easily. They know they're in deep trouble, and I'm the one who has the power to make them face up to it."

Tony stood in the hallway upstairs listening. If there was one thing he knew for certain, it was his father refused to be intimidated by anyone.

"Carol," Frank continued, "I need to do something to make sure they don't ramrod me into losing my job and everything else because I caught them red-handed. I'm going to call WTNN and let them know what's happened. If the news gets ahold of this, at least I'll have something to fall back on. Right now they think I'm the only one they're facing, and I think this needs to be made public."

"But Frank, aren't you afraid it might all just backfire? Can we just pray about this first?"

"Pray? And you think praying will help? Carol, they're already making a move to get rid of me. I've got to stand up and fight before they bury me."

Chapter 19

Tom Driscoll picked up his desk phone on the first ring.

"Yeah, Driscoll here."

Frank wasted no time. "Yeah, my name is Frank Burton. I'm a janitor, or was a janitor, over at the Albright Clinic attached to St. Luke's Hospital."

"Yes," sighed Driscoll, hoping it wasn't just another complaint by a laid-off worker. There were too many of those these days. He was looking for some splashy news item to flash on the screen.

"I found a baby alive today, on my job that they tried to abort in the medical clinic."

"What do you mean, you found a baby?"

"Well, it's like this: every day I do the usual cleaning of the offices in the clinic. Today, when I went into the abortion clinic I heard a baby cry. At first I thought I was hearing wrong. Then I heard it again. I went over to this container on some kind of moving tray and inside was a tiny baby girl."

The shock effect of the news was just what Tom had been waiting for. This item would definitely be a hot one, if it was real. "Where's the baby now?"

"I took it over to the hospital emergency room. Then they airlifted her over to Children's Hospital."

"She's still alive?"

"As of about one hour ago she was."

"What did St. Luke's have to say about it?"

"Well, they wanted to airlift her right away, saying Children's Hospital was the place that could provide the kind of care she needed. But after they found out where she came from everybody started acting real funny. Then this Dr. Joseph Green and a doctor from the hospital got me to go with them up to the clinic where I found her, supposedly to see what I was talking about. Dr. Green was telling them the baby wasn't in his clinic and that he met me in the hallway of the clinic building and tried to help. I couldn't believe it. The guy is totally lying and making this up to cover his butt. So by the time we get to his clinic, the whole thing has been scrubbed and cleaned up. Like nothing ever happened. And now when I got home my wife tells me I got a phone call a little bit ago and my company said I can't go back to work there. The whole thing is a big cover-up. And since they decided to play dirty, I thought I better expose what's going on."

"Well, Frank . . . is it okay if I call you Frank?"

"Yeah, that's fine."

"Frank, I think everybody knows what's going on over there. After all, abortions take place every day."

"Yeah, but do they leave them to die like that?"

"I guess I really don't know what normal procedures are for that."

"Well, do you want the story, or not? If not, I'll call over to KJMP. If you don't want to report it, maybe they will."

"No, just hang on, Frank. I'm sure that was a big shock for you."

"You aren't kidding it was a shock. They just walked off and left her to die. But the wrong guy found her still alive. I told her, and them, I'm not going to leave her. They know I mean business too. Call up to Children's Hospital. Ask them how the little baby that was found at Albright Clinic is doing. The name of the doctor whose office I found her in is Joseph Green."

"Okay. Tell me, where can I reach you?" Tom held the receiver with his shoulder, jotting down the phone number.

"Go ahead and call, and call me back."

"All right. Thanks, Frank."

"And remember, if I don't hear back from you, I'm taking it to another channel that will!" said Frank. He hung up the phone and leaned back in the chair. "So there, Joseph Green. Let's see you try to weasel out of this one."

❧

The Charge Nurse tensed when the man on the phone, Tom Driscoll, said he was with the press.

"Good evening. This is Tom Driscoll with WTNN News. I have information about a baby girl who was brought into your hospital today from St. Luke's. I understand it's a survivor of an abortion at Albright Clinic. Is that true?"

"I'm sorry, sir. I'm not able to release information about any patients, unless you are a direct relation."

"Well, that might be a bit tricky, right? I mean, if it is a baby that survived an abortion, how do we know who its family is?"

"Sir, you're asking questions I am unable to answer."

"Well then, let me talk to a person in charge."

When Gretchen Boyd approached Miles Farber, he knew from the look on her face something was up.

"What is it, Gretchen?"

"Tom Driscoll from WTNN is on the line. He's asking about the little girl brought in today. He wants to know if it's true that she came from the abortion clinic at Albright."

Miles Farber stood back. "No, I'm not going to touch this one. He can call St. Luke's or whoever he wants for all I care, but let them deal with it. I don't want any part of this."

As Gretchen picked up the phone, she took a deep breath.

"Mr. Driscoll, we're unable to answer any questions for you about a patient that is not a family member. There is simply nothing more we can tell you. I'm very sorry."

❧

Joseph Green jumped at the sound of the phone. He was somewhere between a drunken stupor and a dream. He picked it up, anticipating it was his wife wondering where he was.

"Hello."

"Is this Joseph Green?"

"Yeah, who wants to know?"

"Tom Driscoll at WTNN. I'm calling about a report that a baby was recovered from your clinic today and is being treated at Children's Hospital. Can you confirm that for me?"

Joseph Green froze at the news. He knew right away what had taken place. He had hoped forcing Frank off the site would get him to shut up, in fear of losing his job all together. Obviously, that was not the case. Reconsidering, Joseph Green decided to go on the offensive.

"I have nothing to say. You can talk to my attorney."

"Have you personally talked with Mr. Burton about his allegation?"

"Yes, in fact, I have," answered Joseph Green, searching for a way to cut this conversation off. "Burton is a real nutcase.

You know what I mean? I have nothing further to say."

"Dr. Green, are you the doctor in charge of the clinic where Mr. Burton found the child?"

"Again, I have nothing to say. Frank Burton says he found the child in the clinic, but that's a lie. He was out in the hallway of the clinic building acting crazy when I found him. I offered to help, but he just kept pushing me away, saying he would take care of it. I followed him to St. Luke's emergency room. Nothing of what he says is true. For all I know he's part of some crazy scheme by those pro-lifers who everyone knows are just a bunch of fanatics."

"If that were the case, how did they come up with the baby? Are you able to refute the allegations Mr. Burton is making and prove that it wasn't your clinic where he found the child?"

"I am telling you I had nothing to do with it. Now leave me alone!"

"Well, don't you have something to say about your normal procedures as to whether or not such an occurrence would be possible or probable in your practice?"

"I have no comment."

"Anything else you want to tell me, Doc?"

"Nothing except to say we are a well-established clinic that has been in operation in this community for over fifteen years, with no malpractice claims whatsoever. Our track record speaks for itself."

Joseph Green knew he was in a trap. He knew if he refused to talk to them it would appear incriminating for him. He thought of the pro-life activists who had been such a nagging plague to many clinics, and knew if they caught wind of this they wouldn't turn it loose. He also thought of Nancy. What in the world would she do if she found out? She would know right away it was theirs. After all, she was well aware that his patients aborted in their first trimester, and hers was the only one who could have reached the weight this one had. But what choice did he have? Refusal to comment would only fan the flames.

"Doctor Green. Are you still there?" asked Tom, sensing the issues that must be flooding his mind.

"Yeah, I'm here."

"Is there any further comment you would like to make? Our job is to report the news as it comes to us. Do you have any evidence to disprove his statement?"

"As far as I and my clinic are concerned, the burden of proof is on Frank Burton."

"Then I think it only fair to include it in our report."

Knowing he was boxed in, Joseph Green surrendered the whole issue, hoping somehow that nothing would come of it.

"You just remember I will not tolerate any slanderous insinuations from Frank Burton or anyone else regarding the credibility or ethics of me or my practice."

"You've got it, Doc. Thanks for your time."

When he heard the click, Joseph Green knew another door to something uncontrollable had flung open.

Trying to steady his trembling hands, he fumbled to hang up and dropped the phone. If this weren't bad enough what was he going to do about his clinic being featured on the local television station. There was no way in the world he could handle that.

His mind went to his Nancy. "Oh my God, she can't see this." What would she do if she knew her baby was not gone? And what about the baby? He thought he might go out of his mind. How did this ever happen? And Maggie. She'd have his head if anything about Nancy got out. And the clinic! Malpractice! His world cascaded down around him. He had to keep his mouth closed. He hoped Frank Burton would be recognized as the nut-case he was and Nancy wouldn't find out about this. His mind reeled. *What are you hoping for, Joe? Life or death? Are you hoping the little girl will die, Joe? This madness has got to stop.*

Chapter 20

"Dan, we've got a hot one."

"What have you got, Tom?"

"I got a call from a guy named Frank Burton. He's a janitor at the medical building behind St. Luke's. The guy claims he found a live baby in a clinic at the medical building, took it to the ER room at St. Luke's. They airlifted her to Childrens."

"What! What is Childrens saying about it?"

"They're not saying a thing. Won't comment at all. So I called the clinic where the guy says he found the baby. Lo and behold the doctor himself picked up."

"Yeah? What did he have to say?"

"Well, the guy's obviously being real careful. Said Burton was running around like a crazy man in the hallway of the clinic building with a baby. He told me he tried to help but Burton refused. Seems it comes down to one of them is lying. If what Burton says is true and he can prove it, this could take his practice down and he knows it. The guy's scared. Anyway, I want you to give me the go-ahead and send a taping crew to Childrens."

"You know the pro-lifers would love to get ahold of this piece, don't you? This could be a really explosive piece."

"I know. But we've got to move now. Burton's going to call WPMF if we don't get right on it."

"All right. Let me call upstairs and get a crew lined up."

"Thanks, Dan."

Mentally picturing the next morning's headlines, Tom Driscoll mused, *Talk about polarizing issues; this little girl herself was making a statement no one else could make.* "Shaking everybody up, aren't you, baby girl?"

❧

Instantly picking up the phone, he answered, "Driscoll here." He hadn't been this excited about a story they were first to feature in a long time.

"Yeah, Tom, this is Dan. I've got a team out on location now over on the East Side. Do you want them tonight, or do you want to do an early morning piece?"

"Let's do it early morning starting at the clinic. I'll get Burton lined up for that. Then we should have a second team ready at Childrens Hospital. Let's set it for 6:00."

"Sounds good, Tom."

This was the hottest newsbreak Tom Driscoll had handled in his career. The question was: Whose toes were they about to step on? And just how far reaching was this going to be? Recent live footage of Planned Parenthood dealings under the table and the sale of aborted fetuses was still ringing throughout media circles. He knew in his gut this multibillion-dollar industry was one that affected not only personal lives, but on a grander scale also reverberated throughout the medical, political, and business fields. One little baby girl whose life had been mistakenly spared was bringing to light the millions who had been aborted.

Carol Burton watched as Frank answered the call. "Six o'clock? Yeah, that sounds good. I'll be there. I mean, since I'm not going to work tomorrow I've got the whole day." Carol stood by, incredulous. She knew he was stubborn and upset, but this was really getting carried away. She knew she might as well just keep her mouth shut rather than try to dissuade him.

"Okay. I'll meet you in front of Children's at 6:00. Bye." When he hung up, he turned to Carol with a satisfied look.

"Why, Frank?"

"Oh, Carol, you know why. Because I'm not gonna let these people walk all over me, or hide their dirty laundry."

"Yes, but is it for the baby or for you?"

"I guess for both."

"Then I'm going with you in the morning."

"That's fine, Carol, if that's what you want to do."

Underneath it all, her desire was to see the baby for herself and to see this husband of hers exonerated from all the lies being told.

Chapter 21

Nancy Collier sat propped up in bed, coffee cup in hand. She had to go on with her life, now that the abortion was over. There was no going back, and no point stewing in regret. Direction for the future was what she needed now. Direction in her relationship with Joe, and her career. Surfing the channels on the television, she sat back in bed. Seeing a news alert of something at Childrens Hospital, she paused to hear Frank Burton. Explaining that a newborn was rescued from Albright Clinic, sent to St. Luke's, and then airlifted to Childrens Hospital was surreal.

"Has there been contact with the clinic where Mr. Burton allegedly found the newborn?" asked the anchor.

"Colleen, we've contacted a Dr. Joseph Green who operates the clinic, but he has denied any connection to the baby, and declined an interview with us."

"What about the baby girl . . . has her age in terms of the pregnancy been established? And what is her weight?"

"Well, she certainly is a tiny one. Mr. Burton said her weight was recorded at one pound twelve ounces. We estimate the mother was probably twenty-two to twenty-four weeks pregnant."

"Is there a way to be certain Frank Burton's allegations are true, that the child is the product of an unsuccessful abortion? Or is there a possibility she was simply abandoned by someone?"

"Well, we know Frank Burton, who you heard earlier, has been a janitor at the building for fourteen years. Joseph Green, the clinic's physician, is denying any connection."

"What is the baby's current condition?"

"The hospital reports her to be in critical condition, stating survival is questionable, at best."

"Well, thank you, Tom, for this most amazing story. We'll be checking on her progress as the day goes on, and any possible developments as it relates to the clinic."

Nancy knew instinctively it was their daughter. Hearing Joseph Green's denial of responsibility or involvement completely incensed her. Standing up, the adrenaline she felt totally masked any physical weakness she had been experiencing. Nancy wrote Frank Burton's name on a slip of paper next to her phone. She picked up her phone and dialed Joe's cell phone. It went right to voicemail. She immediately called his office. When the answering service picked up, she responded abruptly.

"Tell Dr. Green Nancy called. Tell him I saw the news report and I want to talk to him now. Not later, now!"

Having trouble catching her breath, she knew from past experience that when she encountered severe stress, her body responded in this way. She picked the phone back up and called information.

"Yes, get me Childrens Hospital, please."

Not knowing who to talk to, or what to say, she hung up and headed for her closet. Forget talking. She was going to the hospital.

Chapter 22

Paul switched on the morning news as he sat down to some breakfast. There was some strange report of a local doctor at an abortion clinic and a janitor who found a baby alive.

"Wait a minute. Joseph Green. That's the name on Sheila's medicine bottle. The specialist she said she saw yesterday." Quietly stepping into the bedroom, he picked up the prescription bottle, double-checking to make sure he was right.

"Sheila, wake up!" he demanded. Sheila sat up, rubbing her eyes, trying to clear the sleep away from her mind.

"Who is this doctor you went to see, and what does he do?"

Sheila drowsily tried to respond. "What?"

"Who is this doctor? Who is this Joseph Green? And why is his name on this prescription you brought home with you?" Sheila was horrified that her secret was out.

"Do you know what I just saw on the news? A report about a baby found at an abortion clinic yesterday. And guess what the doctor's name at that clinic was? Joseph Green. Sound familiar, Sheila? Just like the name on this medicine bottle. Joseph Green. I'm not sure I heard you right yesterday. You said you were at some specialist's office. Do you want to explain this to me?"

"Paul, please calm down. I'm sorry. I didn't know what else to do."

"Don't tell me to calm down. You mean you had my baby inside of you and you went and had an abortion?"

"Yes, Paul, I did. I'm sorry. I didn't know what else to do. I didn't think we could handle another kid right now. I thought it was the best thing to do."

"And you didn't come and ask me? Me, the father. You didn't ask me?"

"I didn't want to trouble you with it."

"Trouble me? About a baby! Since when do you not tell me when you're pregnant? And then make a decision like this without me? This is OUR baby, or did you forget that? What gives you the right to keep that from me? This is too much. There's more to this than you're telling me. There has to be. You've never done anything like this without talking to me." "I only did it because I thought it was the best thing to do. I thought it would be best for everybody and if I came to you about it you'd feel obligated for me to have it."

"What! Obligated? Since when have I looked at our kids as an 'obligation'? So you thought you'd just make the decision for both of us without asking me? Let me get this straight. You figured I would want the baby, but because you didn't want it you decided not to 'bother me' with it! Or did you just figure you didn't want it and that's all that mattered? My God. What about the baby? Or did you forget to ask it too?"

Paul stormed out, and Sheila heard the sound of slamming doors and screeching tires. The simple answer she'd sought had vaporized.

"Paul," she said to the wall.

Terror struck her as the realization sank deeper. It was all a huge mistake.

Oh God, let him be back in a little while, she silently prayed.

That morning when the boys woke up, she tried to divert their attention away from Paul not being home as usual.

"Dad had to go in to work early today so he already left. Now go get dressed and I'll get your lunches ready for school."

Her heart was beating out of control. She had to do something. . . . What was he talking about on the news? She switched on the television to see if she could hear the report.

"That's all for this morning's news," she heard. "We'll keep you posted on the baby's condition as we receive updates."

Sheila called the office, letting them know she wouldn't be in today. Looking in the mirror she looked into the eyes of someone she had never known before. The minutes turned into hours as she waited for Paul to pull up. Her heart sank with every passing car. She couldn't recall a moment when she needed him so desperately.

"Why didn't I just tell you the truth?"

Later, after getting the boys off to school, Sheila laid back down to rest. She drifted off until she heard someone calling her name.

"Sheila. Sheila, wake up." It was her sister, Pam, gently shaking her. Sheila sat up in bed, disoriented and confused. As she came to her senses, her sister's presence jolted her with fear.

"Pam, what are you doing here? Is everything okay?" "Obviously things are not okay, Sheila. Paul's at our house. He came over to talk to Gary and me." She looked into her sister's

111

fear-stricken face. "Sheila . . . ," she said, hesitating, searching for the right words. "Paul told us what happened."

Sheila looked at Pam, feeling somehow naked before her. She never intended for anyone else to know what she had done.

After all, it wasn't any of their business. Why was she feeling so ashamed? She was a big girl and she didn't need to defend her own character. She knew what Pam would have to say about this, and she didn't want to hear it.

"Is Paul okay?" she asked, not wanting to address anything directly about herself or what she had done.

"No. He's not okay. He's very upset and confused. Why didn't you tell him what was going on? He's even wondering if there could be another reason why you didn't tell him what was happening."

Sheila's gaze was piercing. "What's that supposed to mean? What 'other' reason would there be?" Their relationship had always been so instinctively close, at times words weren't even necessary. "Come on, Pam, I asked you. What's that supposed to mean?"

"Well, he's wondering if there is more to this than you told him. He said you've been acting real strange for a couple of months." When Pam saw the confusion overtaking Sheila's mind, she continued. "He's wondering if it may have been someone else's baby."

"What!" Sheila retorted. "What are you talking about? I've been pregnant for two months. That's why I've been acting 'strange.' Somebody else's baby! What in the world would make him think such a thing as that? I've never cheated on him. Never. I did this because I thought it would be the best thing for all of us."

"Well, unfortunately you haven't been communicating with him, so he doesn't know what you've been thinking. He said you've never hidden things from him before, and he's wondering if there's more to this. He's in shock, Sheila. He doesn't understand how you could do this, and do it without talking to him about it first. How is he supposed to feel? If it was his baby, then why didn't you talk to him about it?"

The ocean of silence that fell upon them was resounding. Pam knew her point had struck home. She waited for a response.

Sheila stood up and moved toward the window, seeking an escape. She knew deep down her sister loved her. She also knew Pam was forthright enough to make her point known. What she believed to be correct she'd hang on to like a bulldog. There was no arguing the issue with her. She knew Pam was against abortion, and somehow Sheila felt her self-defense slipping away even in her own mind.

The silence that ensued was more difficult to endure than the conversation. "So, big sister, what do you suggest I do? I've already had the abortion. I can't change that. I didn't tell my husband because I thought it would only complicate matters. I can't change that either. So what am I supposed to do? It's over. The baby's gone, and maybe Paul's trust in me is too. But regardless of what he or you or anybody else thinks, I've never cheated on Paul. And the method I chose to deal with this whole thing isn't any of your business."

"Are you okay with it, Sheila?"

"You're not my judge, Pam! I don't have to answer to you. You aren't the one who was pregnant, I was."

When Pam made no response, she continued. "And I sure never thought I'd have to wonder if my own husband believes I'm telling the truth, or how my sister would handle my decision about what I think is a very private issue. In fact, why am I even explaining this to you?"

113

"Sheila, I didn't come over here because you owe me an explanation. I came here because I care about you and about Paul. You made a decision that ended a child's life. And I don't believe it's because you just don't care. I know better, Sheila.

I know you care a lot. But what you did was wrong, and you based your decision on what others believe. Just because so many say it's okay, it's not. Abortion is not right. It is taking a child's life. That baby was part of both you and Paul. And if you're honest with yourself you can see it isn't just the simple cut-and-dried decision everybody says it is. That's the biggest lie of all. It's a herd mentality to keep you from thinking about it too in depth. Like how could so many be wrong? But they are."

"Oh Pam, shut up. What gives you the right to say this to me? Are you Little Miss Perfect? Why don't you just get out of here and leave me alone."

"Sheila, please. I love you and you know it. I love you enough to confront you. This whole thing isn't just going to go away. If you don't deal with this within yourself and with Paul, it's only going to get worse. I know you, Sheila. I know you well enough to know that you did what you did because you thought it was right. But it wasn't. That baby was a real human being. God created that baby and gave it to you as a gift.

He designed it specifically for you and Paul to love."

"Stop it, Pam! Stop it!"

"This won't just go away. Only God can deal with this one.

At best you'll just stuff it deep down inside and with time try to forget about it. But it will always be there until you do deal with it. It's not me who is the judge you need to worry about. It's God. He's the One with the final Word."

"And what is that supposed to mean?" Sheila asked curtly,

as if the question was a challenge to answer what she thought unanswerable. This was all a bunch of nonsense.

"It means that when you figure out this is all too much for you to deal with, God can deal with it. But as long as you think and act as though you're in control and you have the final word, He'll leave it right here with you. He doesn't force Himself on anyone, Sheila. He just makes Himself available to everyone. The choice remains with you but the final word is always His."

Again silence fell. As Pam reached out to touch her, Sheila pulled back.

"You know what, Pam, you just have to try to prove how right you are, don't you? I just made one of the most difficult decisions of my life. What makes you think I need you coming over here to tell me how wrong I am? I'm tired of it. I haven't done anything but try to do my best for my family. And if that doesn't measure up to what you think is 'right,' too bad. Only this is between my husband and me. This is our personal business, and I'll thank you to back off."

As the words sank deep into her heart, Pam felt herself choking inside. She really didn't come to judge. Why couldn't Sheila see that? Seeing the coldness on Sheila's face let her know there was no more to be said. She had to let go. The deeper truth she wanted Sheila to know was that God wouldn't judge her either if she would just admit it was wrong. Taking back the past is impossible, but the only way to overcome it was by surrendering to the Lord and confessing it for what it was. Sin and death.

"Sheila, it has taken me over twenty years to come to the place of understanding that God doesn't condemn us. He forgives us. In fact, I believe even your baby forgives you. Those babies have eternal spirits that go on living. And I believe with all my heart the Lord takes them into His arms with love and care, and He also loves and cares about their mothers. Yes, even mothers who abort them. When the babies go to be with Him, I honestly believe He and the babies are reaching out for their mothers. He didn't die for good people. There aren't any good people in the world. We're all sinners and He died for every one of us. And that forgiveness is for every sin we commit; past, present, and future. If that weren't true, none of us would have a chance. He died for every sin, regardless of whether we accept His forgiveness or not. But we have to believe in Him and accept what He's already done for us. I couldn't find peace about the baby we lost eight years ago if it weren't for me believing that baby isn't dead. It's waiting for the moment we enter heaven too. I know many Christians and churches have been hard on women who have gone through this. For that, I am truly sorry. But anyone honest enough to look at themselves knows we're all in the same boat. Truth be told, Jesus made it pretty clear when He said, 'Let him who is without sin cast the first stone.' No such person exists."

Chapter 23

Sheila's heart beat rapidly. As the garage door closed, her mind raced with imaginings of what Paul's attitude would be. All she knew was she wanted their marriage back on good terms.

After Paul closed the door behind him and looked into her eyes, Sheila cried, "Oh, Paul. I am so sorry. But you've GOT to believe me. I have NEVER cheated on you. NEVER. I didn't know what to do. I just got so overwhelmed with the thought of having another baby. I never would have done it if I thought it would tear us apart."

"You know what, Sheila? I forgive you. Even for this. But I will never understand why you didn't tell me."

"I just thought it would be better if I didn't. It seemed like the easiest way of dealing with it."

Silence fell as she looked into his eyes. He had always been good to her. Yes, there were rocky times in their relationship, as in any. But he had always been good to her.

"If I had known how you were going to react, I never would've done it, Paul. I thought we were through having children. The boys are getting older, and my job has made things easier. We've been able to do so many more things since I started working. It just seemed like starting all over would be too hard."

"I don't know what to say, Sheila. I forgive you. But I guess I just don't understand how you could have done what you did."

"I just did it. That's all. I found out I was pregnant, and the day I did, they asked me to let them know what I wanted to do. At first I didn't think I had a choice. But when the subject came up, it just seemed to be the way out. I was only two months along."

"I want you to go see the doctor. I want you to find out what our options are for making sure this doesn't happen again. If it's something I should do, then I'll do it. But I don't ever want this to happen again."

"Okay, Paul. I'll talk to him."

"Let's put this behind us now and get on with our lives. That is, if you're telling the truth and want to go on."

"Of course I do, Paul. That's what I've always wanted. Pam told me what you had to say. Oh, Paul, don't ever doubt my faithfulness to you. There isn't and never has been anyone else."

As she said it, the thought raced through her mind, *Faithful? But Mommy, what about me?* She fought to focus on what she was saying to Paul. She just wanted this whole thing over with so life could get back to normal. Nothing else mattered.

"I guess I thought Pam would know what was going on with you . . . especially if there was a problem between us. I didn't go to listen to them rant and rave about their religious stuff." As he said it, he knew in his heart he was exaggerating. Pam and Gary hadn't said anything out of place.

"What did Pam say when she came over here?"

"Oh, I don't know. She was talking about 'God is the only judge.' I hate it when she starts in. It's like she's the only one on the face of the earth that's ever been through anything, and her way is the only way. She doesn't understand half as much as she thinks she does. She's never been in my shoes."

Sheila hardened herself to her thoughts of Pam. *You know she really cares about you, Sheila.* Putting her hands to her head, she tried once again to stop the thoughts. First it was the baby, then Paul . . . now Pam. Feeling the tightness in her stomach, she silently longed for the passing of time to bring distance from it all. *This has got to get better with time, doesn't it?* she wondered.

"Paul, I promise you, I'll never make a decision such as this again without first talking to you about it."

"I hope not, Sheila. I don't think I could deal with this again. We'll put it behind us. But I have to know you're not doing things behind my back. We have to be able to trust one another, Sheila."

"Yes, Paul. I know. How well I know."

Chapter 24

*N*ancy Collier rushed past the nurse's station, heading directly to ICU.

On guard with orders following the morning news broadcast, the Charge Nurse called to her. "Miss, can I help you?" Nancy ignored her.

"Miss. May I help you?"

Nancy stopped and turned. "Yes, the baby. The baby girl who was on the news, she's mine. She's my baby. I want to see her. I want to see her now."

Looking over her shoulder, Paula Birch gave a signal to another nurse on duty to go get help. The number of calls they had received since the early morning broadcast was unreal. They had been warned that there might even be people attempting to enter the ward to see the baby. They were given strict orders that no one was to be allowed in to see her.

"I'm sorry, Miss. Our policy restricts unauthorized visitations."

"Sorry, lady, but a mother isn't under the guise of 'Restricted or Unauthorized' visitors," Nancy retorted.

"I'm sorry, Miss. I'm afraid I'll have to ask you to stop."

"Well, then, call Dr. Joseph Green at the women's clinic at

Albright. He knows who I am, and he can attest to me being the mother of this baby. Tell him Nancy Collier is here, demanding to see her baby. He'll know who I am."

"If you want to have a seat in the waiting room, I'll see what I can do."

Just then Frank and Carol Burton exited the elevator.

Unhesitatingly, Frank led the way toward the ICU.

Recognizing him from the news broadcast earlier, Paula knew she was in need of help. Not only did she have to attempt to hold this woman at bay, but now Frank Burton was back. Attempting to keep the two apart, she turned to Nancy.

"Come with me, Miss Collier, and I'll try to reach Dr. Green for you."

Nancy spotted Frank, and headed toward him, totally ignoring Paula's attempt to sidetrack her.

"Mr. Burton? Frank Burton?"

"Yes, I'm Frank Burton."

"Mr. Burton, I'm Nancy Collier. I saw you on the morning news and I rushed right over here. Mr. Burton, can you tell me again exactly what happened yesterday?"

Paula Birch tried to interrupt the conversation. When both Nancy and Frank ignored her attempts, she stepped in abruptly. "Excuse me, Mr. Burton, but I'll have to ask you to leave."

"Oh, you will, will you? Well, you can 'ask' me to leave, but I'm not going to," answered Frank.

"I have direct orders that you are not to be allowed up here."

"According to who?"

"According to those in authority here."

"Hey, wait a minute, lady. Yesterday when I brought this baby in I was told by your own Dr. Hanson that I wouldn't have any problem checking on her."

"I'm sorry, Mr. Burton. I'm just following orders."

"Well, I'll tell you what, call whoever gave you orders and tell them I'm not going anywhere. I'm staying right here."

Not knowing how to defuse the situation, Paula took a step back.

"All right, Mr. Burton. But I'll have to ask you to have a seat in our waiting room while I try to reach someone."

Walking away, she knew that she had to let go of any attempt to control Frank Burton. This was all getting way out of hand. After all, she was a nurse, not a policewoman. If Joseph Green was responsible for all this, then Joseph Green could deal with it.

Carol put her hand on Frank, attempting to calm him.

"C'mon, Frank. Let's go sit down and wait until she comes back."

"Mr. Burton," asked Nancy, "please talk to me."

"Well, I'll talk to you if you want the truth."

"Yes, Mr. Burton. The truth is exactly what I want."

Nancy sat immobilized as Frank went over the facts of the day before. When he finished recalling the events leading up to the emergency room, he looked at Nancy with wonder. "Why are you so interested in this?"

"Well, you have to understand something," she began. "I was at Dr. Green's clinic yesterday, and I had an abortion. I have every reason to believe she's my baby. I was in my second trimester of pregnancy, and I know most of the women who have abortions are much earlier in their pregnancies than I was. I believe that she's my baby."

"Well, isn't that interesting. The good doctor is denying I found the baby in his clinic and saying I'm making this all up. When he and I went with another doctor from the hospital so I could retrace my steps and show them where I found her, the clinic was all cleaned up as if the containers and equipment I had found vanished."

Frank and Carol looked at one another in disbelief. How in the world could all this be happening? Bad enough Tony was involved in the whole thing. Then Frank's job. And now this?

"I can't imagine what you saw. That must have been a horrifying experience for you. But when I heard you on the news this morning, I had to come. I had to be here. I couldn't just walk away from this. It was hard enough to make the decision I made, but knowing my baby is in there fighting for her life, I had to come." Carol reached over and tried to console Nancy.

Just then a nurse stepped into the room where the Burtons and Nancy were waiting."

"Mr. Burton?"

"Yes, I'm Frank Burton."

"Mr. Burton, I've been given permission to inform you the baby continues to be in critical condition. Because of hospital rules regarding visitors, you may call our nurse's desk throughout the day to check on her status if you'd like, but we're unable to let you see her. She then turned to Nancy and asked, Miss Collier?"

"Yes, I'm Nancy Collier."

"Miss Collier can you please follow me?"

Nancy rose and followed her out and down the corridor further into the ICU. The nurse then stopped and opened a door to another waiting room. She entered and held the door for Nancy to follow.

"Miss Collier, Dr. Green would like you to wait, if you would. He said he'd be here in approximately thirty minutes."

"Yes, I'll wait. But in the meantime, I want to see my baby."

"Dr. Green wants you to wait until he gets here."

"I'm not going to wait for him. I don't care what he wants!"

"I'll have to check for you. I was just asked to have you wait for Dr. Green."

"What about the Burtons?" Nancy asked.

"As I told them, they are allowed to call in for status updates, but they will not be allowed into the patient's room."

Nancy felt her anger rise. She then walked past the nurse and back out into the hall. She continued until she returned to the room where she had met the Burtons and reentered.

"They're asking me to wait for Dr. Green in another room," she explained.

"Well, I hope you find yourself a new doctor after all this," said Frank. "The guy is a real case," he continued. "Bad enough I found the baby there, but then he has the nerve to pull a fast one and get everything cleaned up and say he has no idea what I'm talking about and that I'm a liar."

Not ready to divulge the extent of her relationship with Joseph Green, she felt the need to keep quiet.

Carol stepped forward, once again gently hugging Nancy.

"If we can be of help in any way, please let us know."

"Thank you. I will."

Paula Birch entered and turned to Nancy. "If you would follow me, please Miss Collier."

Nancy followed her lead, not knowing Joseph Green had arrived and was waiting for her in the other room.

After Nancy left, Frank turned and asked Carol, "Why are you being so nice to that woman? She's one of them, Carol. Don't you get it?"

"No, Frank. She's not just 'one of them.' She's obviously a woman who was desperate and didn't know what else to do. We don't know what she's dealing with."

Joseph Green sighed with relief when Paula Birch whispered

to him the Burtons were on their way out. She then held the door for Nancy to enter. Closing the door behind her, she had to admit this was one of the most bizarre situations they had handled in her ten years at Children's.

Chapter 25

Joseph Green took a deep breath and smiled as he came face to face with Nancy.

"Hi, Nancy."

When their eyes met, he was unable to speak. Nancy knew the silence to be the confirmation she expected.

"Why didn't you tell me?"

"Tell you what?"

"Oh, no. We're not going to play games, Joe."

Afraid of someone overhearing, he quietly closed the door.

"You know exactly what I mean. She's our baby."

"Nancy, what are you talking about? That crazy nutcase on the news? That Burton fellow? He's a raving lunatic."

"I just met him, as you probably have already been told. Somehow I get the impression he's a real honest kind of guy, and not a 'raving lunatic' as you call him."

"I don't know any such thing."

"You know she's ours, don't you? No one else who came to you yesterday was as far along as me, were they?"

"No, I don't believe so. But that doesn't prove she's ours, Nancy. He's making up that whole story about finding her in the clinic."

Nancy stood up and looked him straight in the eyes. "When are you gonna stop, Joe? When are you gonna be real? Are you even going to deny she's your own daughter?"

When he failed to answer, she knew it was pointless.

"I am her mother, Joe. Even if you're not willing to admit you're her father, I'm not going to deny her. You do whatever it is you feel you need to do, and I will do what I know I have to. As far as I'm concerned it's all over between us. Right now, I want to see my baby! I'll have my stuff out of the apartment as soon as I possibly can."

Just then Joseph Green heard an emergency page. He looked at her and said, "I'll tell them to let you in to see her, Nancy. I love you."

"No, Joe. No you don't. I don't know if you even have the capacity to love. In fact, I think Frank Burton knows a whole lot more about love than you."

There were no words that could condemn his manhood more than those. As he turned to go and opened the door, Paula Birch returned asking, "Dr. Green, may I speak with you for a moment please? Out in the hall and under her breath she whispered, "She's gone, doctor. We lost her just a minute ago."

Halted by the news, he turned and looked at Nancy.

Instantly, she knew.

Tears welled up in her eyes.

"She's gone, isn't she?"

Joe took a step forward, in an attempt to console her. She pushed him aside and stepped back.

"Don't touch me. Where is she?"

Paula looked at him, wondering what to do.

"Let her in, Paula. Let her see the baby."

Knowing he could not handle the two of them coming

127

together, Joseph Green turned to leave. As Nancy watched him walk away, she wondered what she had ever seen in him. Her passion for him was now just disgust and resentment. Paula led the way to the crib, uncovered the body, and stepped back.

Cries of sorrow resonated throughout the ward.

Chapter 26

Kneeling before the small gravestone, face buried in her hands, Nancy Collier continued to mourn. Her eyes, full of sorrow and tears, came to rest on the engraving:

Rosebud Collier
Born: April 17
Died: April 18
Daughter of Nancy M. Collier
"A life to be lived beyond the gate."

As a hand came to rest on her shoulder, she turned. Carol Burton knelt beside her and embraced her. "Oh, Nancy. It's true. She really is living beyond the gate." Frank stood by, looking on.

"Oh, God, I hope so," responded Nancy.

"In fact, I know of two little ones right now who are hoping to see us all someday."

Nancy looked at her in confusion. "Two?"

"Believe it or not, our own grandchild was aborted the same day, Nancy. We didn't know it at the time, but one of the others aborted in the clinic that day was our own grandchild. My son got a girl pregnant and she went to the same place for an abortion that morning."

"Oh, my God. What are we all doing? We have to stop this from happening."

Carol held Nancy close.

"She'll never know what you did, Nancy. God has wiped away all her pain and agony, and she'll never know anything but joy and peace. She still loves you too. And she wants to someday have the opportunity to be held by you."

"How? How could that be possible? I'm responsible for her death!"

"She doesn't know that, Nancy. And she never will. The only thing she'll know is that you're her mother, and she wants to be with you."

"I don't think that's possible. I never even gave her a chance to live. Why would she want to know me?"

"Why does any child want to know its mother? Simply because you are her mother. Whether she's alive here on earth or alive with the Lord, she's still your daughter."

"Well, that'll be real tricky. I hardly think I'll be where she is."

"Believe it or not, that's a choice you have the opportunity to make. Jesus didn't die for perfect people, you know. He died for all the sins of the world. We just have to believe in Him, accept His forgiveness, and accept His love."

Continuing, Carol said, "Nancy, can I share with you a scripture that keeps coming to mind at this moment?"

Nancy just affirmatively nodded.

Carol continued, "Nancy, Rosebud, as well as all babies who died by abortion were knit together by God Almighty Himself. None of them are overlooked or forgotten. And not only that He loves and forgives you. That is probably the toughest thing for any of us to believe and actually accept. He forgives us all. The worst as well as the best. He loves you and forgives you. Not just a little bit, but completely. Perfect little Rosebud, and imperfect Nancy, her mother. He didn't just die for the good people, but for the whole world. It's not about us. It's about Him and how good He really is."

"Well, that's pretty hard to believe. Why would He love me and want to forgive me?"

"I guess that's the biggest mystery of all. Because we're all part of the humankind that He created. I believe Rosebud loves you and wants you too. She doesn't remember what the end of her life was like, or who was responsible. When life here is over, we're either soaking in all the greatness of His Presence or we're separated and left in torment because we didn't accept what He freely offered. He says He'll wipe away all of our tears once we leave this world if we put our trust in Him."

"Well then at least I know she's okay," mused Nancy.

"Then take it a step further, Nancy,' Carol continued. 'Rosebud wants her mother. She wants to feel your embrace and know the one who carried her. All you have to do is believe you too can be forgiven."

Second Chronicles 7:14 says, "If My people who are called by My name shall humble themselves, pray, seek, crave and require of necessity My face, and turn from their wicked ways, then will I hear from Heaven, forgive their sin, and heal their land."

Obscured from view by the surrounding evergreens, Joseph Green looked on. He had cancelled his morning appointments, explaining he had a funeral to attend. Watching the exchange that was taking place between Nancy and the Burtons, he experienced an even deeper emptiness within. As he looked at them, he wondered, *Are they right about me? Am I ever going to find peace and happiness again?*

Looking toward the sky he cried, "Okay, God! What do You want from me?

As clear as day he heard, "Admit what you've become, Joe, and ask Me to come in and change you!"

Epilogue

Passing through a tunnel surrounded by the stars of the heavens, they were drawn by a power that was undeniable. The source radiated light so powerful its rays stretched into eternity. Those who died before birth heard voices while still in their mothers' wombs and were mysteriously aware of life going on about them. Floating in their warm, secure surroundings, suddenly, without warning, each was thrust into an agony of pain and torment beyond description. Injections of saline solution burned their flesh. They were suctioned out, shredded into pieces, or extracted with instruments in the hands of skilled personnel. If still intact and delivered whole, the base of their skulls and brain stems were severed to bring instant death. Unknown to those sacrificing their babies, the human remains were often packaged and sold off to laboratories for research and undisclosed uses.

They cried out, but no one heard. The solitude and silence they lived in concealed their torment. The mothers who succumbed to the procedures in desperation psychologically separated themselves from their inward existence. Their cries fell silent within the barrier of the wombs they were conceived in. But God heard their cries.

So alone and unnoticed in death, their families didn't mourn as one would for a child. They were the discarded of self-centered lifestyles that valued convenience and personal ambition more than human life itself. They were not only put to death before they were given a glimpse of the world they grew toward entering, but after death many bodies and parts were actually sold for use in science labs or used as product ingredients for modern-day cosmetics. It was the most horrific modern-day Holocaust, actually legislated and refused recognition in clinics and hospitals all over the world. There were no funerals signifying the end of their lives on earth. Not even mass graves were prepared. Rather, their bodies were sold in the marketplace.

No single government or party lay claim to this. It was a genocide of universal proportions. Population control labeled in a manner conducive to its immediate surroundings. In the United States and Europe it was a matter of "choice." In China it was demanded by the government of all who already had one child, and called "good" for the sake of the masses who must be fed. For those killed, it was a torment of untold pain and agony.

The value in the eyes of the One who created them was completely unrecognized. The God of Love had determined to save them even before they existed. He bought them with His Son's own body and blood, paying the highest price conceivable. It was the sacrifice of His Son for all. Even those who slew them.

As suddenly as their torment had begun, it stopped. They instantly became part of a continual trail of people undeniably drawn into a great light. Babies, children, adults alike moved swiftly along. The wonder of the Power drawing them was even more awe inspiring than what immediately surrounded them. Those who knew Him on earth were filled with an anticipation each had felt since their new birth into the kingdom. The babies knew nothing of what compelled them. The underlying glory of it all resided in the reality of God's love for them. His love reached in and surpassed the indifference with which mankind had responded to those slain. His love took their death and trans-formed it into eternal life. Though no one else knew them, He knew them from the beginning of time.

Though their lives were overlooked and forsaken by mankind, God had a plan. Each had a purpose He foreordained for them to discover and enjoy, a purpose with meaning and fulfillment. Their lives were just beginning, and they would be used solely for God's plan. They would no longer be forsaken. They had been redeemed. It was the commencement of God's plan for them.

Their absence from the earth in body by no means meant the absence of their effect on those left behind. Even those responsible for their deaths would be reached out to and touched in a way only He knew. Just as He was able to take their deaths and give them life in return, He would use the heartache of those responsible, whose consciences weren't completely seared, and bring them salvation. It was the wonder of a God whose ability and goodness were time and again expressed and measured by and in those who were set free. Only His perfect love went beyond their sin. It was the only thing that brought hope where there was none, and gave joy in exchange for the pain of living in a world riddled with hurt and confusion.

Continuing to move toward the Power that drew them, angels surrounded them. The angels were rejoicing in the knowledge of the One whose presence they were about to behold. They were a heavenly escort, sent to usher God's people into their land of promise.

The Father awaited each entry with great expectation. The

moment He continually dreamed of arrived each time a new child of His entered His presence. Both they and He knew the joy that filled their hearts, but only He knew the joy that it brought Him. Each individual was a continual reminder to Him that the price He paid was rewarded with another's life. He had known them each from the moment of their conception. And now His greatest delight was to be able to reveal Himself to them completely, unhindered. It was the moment when each came face to face with Him and found intimate friendship with God.

As they continued toward the Light, a huge gate appeared before them. It was the great gate of pearl. Passing through, they discovered the Light was drawing them to the very Throne of God.

Entering His presence, the rays became a blended part of the radiance all about Him. All fell down before His throne. The power of His holiness was indescribable. Their beings exploded with His presence. Life had found its source. The Living God was before them. The angels sang, "Holy, Holy, Holy is the Lord God Almighty, who was and is and forevermore shall be." Their beings were bowed with reverence. They were speechless as His glory surrounded them.

Restfully sitting before them, He spoke, "Rise up, My children, and call Me blessed. For My reward is great. I have desired to bring you each into My presence. In Me is fullness of joy. Drink deep of My presence. Know that I have redeemed you for Myself. You are My chosen ones. Let all who know Me rejoice, for My joy I give unto you. My peace has become your inheritance. My presence shall forever surround you and we shall never again be separated or distant. We shall live together continually now and forevermore.

"Rise now and see, your King sits beside Me. He is My true Crown of Glory. There is none other like Him, for We are

One. It is His blood that is here before Me, giving you access to My throne. It is He who paid the price that you might dwell with Me. So open your eyes and behold Him now. His majesty is displayed in His presence and He desires for you to know Him. Come before Him now with thanksgiving, for He is your Redeemer and King."

As they lifted their heads to gaze upward, the drawing power of His majesty took hold of them. He was there before them in person. The Lion of the Tribe of Judah sat upon His Throne. His eyes were of fire; His presence fanned the flames. His unfeigned love and gentleness emanated toward them as He called them near.

"Let me look at you. Come close, My beloveds. For I knew you the moment you were conceived, and have hungered for this moment. I have so desired to meet you face to face. You are home now, and we welcome you. Your life shall now be as it was meant to be. For you were created in Our image to rule and reign. And what was known only as a shadow of things to come in the earth shall now be revealed to you in full splendor. For you shall forevermore rule and reign with Me.

"You shall come to know and understand fully the role of kingship and priesthood, which you were created to possess. For you shall rule in the heavens and the earth under My command and you shall serve Me in the royal priesthood which My blood has made the way for. For I know the plans I have for you. You shall be taught and instructed by My Spirit, for there is much yet to be done on the earth.

"Those of you who are unknown to them shall become known as restorers of the breach. For many of you have been cast away by the people of the earth, but you shall all be with Me to gather them together with your prayers uttered here in

My kingdom, and with your arms when the moment arrives for them to come Home.

"You will each be taken to your own dwelling place. Many have rooms which at present are empty. You will each fill them with your prayers. Prayers filled with the faith of My Spirit. That faith is the substance of those individuals yet remaining in the earth who are destined to join us in My kingdom. Again I welcome you. I rejoice in your arrival. Now go and behold the place I have prepared for you."

Dancing along the path to the Great Hall, bird songs filled Rosebud's heart. She stooped to pick a few flowers. There were so many to choose from, it was hard to know when to stop. Their colors were so extravagant and lovely. They grew in perfect harmony, as did all things that her eyes beheld.

"Father, may I have a pretty gold vase for these when I reach the Great Hall? Thank you. I better hurry; there's so much to do. I praise you, Father that the flowers shall always be here for me to enjoy. I'd like to place this bouquet on my table if I may. The colors are so wonderful."

The Grand Celebration was approaching, and the very thought of it made her feel she could skip in air. She didn't understand why she felt such excitement about it. After all, she had never experienced an event such as this.

Maybe it was seeing all the others working busily at each of the tasks they had been assigned. All working toward what they had been promised would be a day so glorious they couldn't even imagine. What could be better than this? After all, everything was already glorious. Everything she experienced was full of wonder and excitement. Times of worship to the Father were unsurpassed, and times of seeing and speaking to Jesus, well, what more could there be?

Rosebud's eyes twinkled with joy as she thought of the first moment she learned of the Grand Celebration. She knew some of the places at the various tables were marked for those who were in the kingdom, yet still on earth. She had only memories of an existence of warmth and darkness.

She had heard that many of those on the earth didn't know the Lord and were not going to be coming to heaven. It was impossible for her to understand how those who did not know Him chose to live separate from Him. It made no sense to her whatsoever. How anyone could not want Him she would never understand. He was life, joy, kindness, and peace, all the good things that flourished within her. How could anyone choose to exist without Him?

"Thank you, Lord that I'll never exist like that. I thank You, Lord, that You chose me, and I'll be with you forever." You are the most wonderful surprise of all, she thought. Knowing You, loving You, and worshiping You. The river of life within her rose to a level that flooded all else each time she stopped to think of Him. There was nothing more important than being in His presence. Nothing!

When the worship reached its highest crescendo, their voices rose as a wave uncontainable. They became the sound of heaven.

"I love You, Father," she whispered.

"And I love you, child," she heard Him reply. When the wave receded she heard Him speak again.

"Now let's prepare our celebration."

"Yes, Father," she happily replied.

Entering the Great Hall, she pondered the thought that even the Father was going to be celebrating. Thousands of years had passed in anticipation of this moment. The bride of Christ was soon coming home.

Rosebud blushed as the angels all around began to laugh with glee. Joy unspeakable and full of glory.

"Father, bring the others here to be with us. Send messengers across their paths to bring them here, and please make sure my mother is one of them."

*

"Although my father and my mother have forsaken me,
yet the Lord will take me up (adopt me as His child)."
(Psalm 27:10 AMP).

"When I passed by you again and looked upon you,
indeed your time was the time of love; so I spread My wing
over you and covered your nakedness. Yes, I swore an oath
to you and entered into a covenant with you,
and you became Mine," says the Lord God.
(Ezekiel 16:8 NKJV)

Beyond the Gate of Mercy and Grace
From the mouth of the Lord comes a call.
Come unto Me, My children;
Draw near to Me and see;
My love poured out so freely
So My glory all can see.